ARMED INSTINCT

By Brett Hoeppner

CHAPTER 1
HEAD FIRST

A sudden thud echoed through the abandoned public restroom as the broken fluorescent light gently swayed on the ceiling. The bluish light flickered as a battered and beaten Carlton slid down the wall of broken tiles in between two urinals. The skinny weasel of a man blinked the blood from his eyes in an attempt to gain his bearings. Grayson's leather jacket whipped behind him as he cocked the hammer of his stainless-steel revolver and drove the barrel in between Carlton's eyes. Thick blood filled the dry cracks in Grayson's knuckles as his fingers tightened around the grip of his shiny hand-cannon.

"The code," Grayson demanded through gritted teeth.

"You think death scares me anymore?" Carlton giggled in a smart-ass tone.

Grayson, without looking, moved the muzzle of the .44 magnum down to the alligator-skin loafer on Carlton's right foot. A blinding muzzle flash lit up the room as bits of flesh and leather pelted Carlton's bony face along with a sprinkle of his own blood. Carlton glanced at what remained of his foot and couldn't stifle a panicked screech as tears emerged from the corners of his shaky eyes.

"Death may not scare you, but it looks like pain still does," Grayson stated.

The report of the magnum echoed down the hall, through the exit, and into the quiet darkness of the deserted city streets. Next to the open doorway leading into the hall, Faith was leaning her back against the building with a single foot resting on the wall behind her. The echoed blast met her ears and she readied herself by popping her katana an inch out of its glossy black sheath. Her sharp eyes darted to the hallway.

As she squinted, listening intently, her crow's feet began to wrinkle under her smoky eye shadow. The leather wrapping on the katana's hilt gently crunched as her grip tightened. Once she heard the distant voice of Grayson, she released her grip and let gravity pull the blade back into its scabbard with a "clack." Her fitted leather jacket creased as she crossed her arms and rested her head against the rough, stucco exterior wall. As Carlton's scream danced down the hall and met her ears, she sighed and began to nibble on her lower lip. She scanned the worn-down street in front of her with only flickering street lights to guide her sight in the darkness.

In the bathroom, Grayson crouched down to eye-level with the wounded Carlton who was gripping his ankle and panting. Revolver in hand, Grayson patted down his own pockets in search of something. His aged eyes focused as he reached his front right pocket.

"Here we go," Grayson proclaimed as he revealed the item.

Grayson held up a black Microtech automatic knife and stared at it for a moment.

"Wrong thing. Here, hold this for a second,"

With his calloused thumb, he pressed the switch and a polished serrated blade instantly extended from the knife body. He then flipped the knife around and casually stabbed it into the bloody stump that used to be Carlton's foot. Carlton wretched and gargled with pain as his eyes began to roll into the back of his head.

"Come on now, Carlton. Stay with me here," Grayson said through a rageful scowl while he briefly shook Carlton's other foot. Carlton managed to catch himself from losing consciousness but whimpered like an injured dog.

Grayson confidently slid his hand into his jacket pocket and removed a colorful child's bracelet with the name "*Emily*" spelled out with alphabet beads.

"This look familiar?"

"Grayson, it… it isn't… I didn't…" Carlton stuttered.

"Sorry, forgot you had this," Grayson stated as he removed the blade from Carlton's stub, twisting it on the way out. He dodged a squirt of blood that shot from the stump as he pulled the knife from the wound.

Grayson wiped the bloody knife on Carlton's tacky slacks, retracted the blade and pocketed it. Carlton began banging the back of his head on the bathroom wall while squealing like a hyena.

"Shit, I should have mentioned that the bracelet came with this," Grayson removed a crumpled piece of paper from his jacket pocket. As he unfolded it and pulled it tight, a single hand-written word revealed itself in red ink. *Carlton*. A red stamp featuring the silhouette of a crow's head encircled with barbed wire rested in the bottom right corner of the paper.

"That's bullshit, man. BULLSHIT!" Carlton desperately spat through bloodied teeth. "That old man doesn't know shit!"

"I don't want to hear anything come out of your mouth other than a fucking code!" Grayson retorted.

"Fuck you, Grayson! All I ever did was look out for you! You don't even *know* what I did for you! I kept you and Faith ALIVE!"

Emotionless, Grayson pointed the short barrel of his Smith and Wesson revolver at Carlton's other foot.

"The code!" Grayson demanded as he covered Carlton's remaining foot with the orange front sight sitting atop the barrel of his firearm.

"Fuck y-"

BOOM! Carlton's foot split in two as his toes skidded across the floor. As he watched his last functioning foot get blown apart by Grayson, he reached for the urinal next to him in a primal attempt to crawl away.

"The code!"

BOOM! Carlton's skinny righthand wrist shredded to bits and his hand dangled by a string of meat. The bullet also struck the urinal causing porcelain fragments to explode throughout the bathroom.

"The code!"

BOOM! The silver band on Carlton's left ring finger shattered. His severed finger hit the ceiling and plopped into a toilet bowl. Bits of silver were embedded in Carlton's gaunt cheek and neck. He began to screech hysterically from the sight of his mutilated extremities as the shock started to wear off and the pain began to truly set in.

"THE CODE!"

Grayson cocked the hammer with his thumb; the cylinder of the revolver rotated and locked in place. His finger, now covered in blood, hovered over the trigger. The sights aligned over Carlton's crotch and smoke rose from the crown of the barrel.

"THE CODE, CARLTON!" Grayson screamed with spittle flying from his fiery lips.

Outside, Faith rhythmically tapped her slender fingers on the sleeve of her jacket. She quickly snapped her head up at the sound of footsteps shuffling through the loose asphalt in front of her. Three shifty men in ragged attire casually and confidently loomed on the edge of the darkness in front of her.

"You okay over here?" shouted the leader of the grungy men as he pushed his tongue into his cheek.

"We heard some gunshots and wanted to make sure everything was okay," he continued as he and his friends closed in.

Although the approaching men wore tattered street-garb, they projected an innocent and helpful air. They looked at each other as they approached, curious as to why she ignored them.

"I said, are you okay?" the leader repeated as he moved his hand behind his back.

They were mere feet away from Faith when the leader revealed his hand which brandished a chipped and rusted machete. He opened his mouth as if to threaten her, but before any noise left his lips, he saw his own hand floating in front of him. It still gripped the machete, but at the wrist was an exposed cluster of bones and dangling tendons. Confused, he saw three glints of light followed by his fingers separating from his hand. His severed fingers bounced off the ground like baby carrots as the machete clanked on the asphalt and a spray of blood peppered his eyes causing him to flinch.

Faith still leaned calmly against the wall of the building with a crooked bathroom sign resting near her head. A faint "*click*" echoed from her sheath as her sword came to rest in its home. The man grabbed his wrist as globs of blood fell from his meaty nub. He began to grunt in stifled agony until he saw Faith put her finger to her lips and shushed him. She then pointed at graffiti on the wall next to her. The words "LEAVE NOW" were spray-painted in bright red. The man held his groans of pain as his two henchmen stood paralyzed in fear and disbelief. Begrudgingly, she uncrossed her arms and pushed herself off the wall.

Faith took a few steps, her boots clacking on the asphalt beneath her, and leaned against the wall directly underneath the restroom sign. On the wall, where she had been standing, was another message in bright red spray paint: "FUCK OFF." She shrugged and shooed them away with her hand.

"Kill the bitch!" The leader shakily screamed as his eyes began to flicker away from consciousness.

One of the goons pulled a meat cleaver from his waistband and the cardboard sheath that was holding it fell to the ground. Faith took two strides toward him and, in a single motion, unsheathed her katana and slashed the blade of the meat cleaver in half. The top half of the cleaver flew into the wounded leader's neck with a squishy thud, knocking him to the ground. The other hoodlum drew a rusted revolver from his jacket and raised the firearm to eye-level. Faith turned to face him and stared right down the brown barrel of the gun.

"Nighty-night, bitch," the filthy man said through a grin of missing teeth.

He pulled the trigger, the hammer cocked and released, rotating the cylinder.

"Click."

Faith tilted her head to the side; unsurprised at the firearm's malfunction. His smile dropped and he turned the gun to inspect it closer. Faith gracefully pierced the man's gun-hand with her sword, continued to push through his mouth, and the tip of the sword popped out the back of his head. A wispy moan eked through his open mouth as he looked, in horror, at Faith's emotionless expression.

The other henchman charged at Faith from behind with the bottom half of his meat cleaver as he let out a pathetic war cry. Faith removed the sword from the man's head, causing his dead weight to collapse to the ground, and whipped the blade at the charging goon, spraying blood into his eyes. The guy let out a yelp and turned his head away from the spray of blood. Faith, with two smooth slashes, lopped the man's arms off causing him to release a guttural scream. His body twisted and fell to the ground as the back of his head landed on the crumbling curb of the nearby sidewalk.

Faith pressed her boot into the man's bloody jacket and rolled his body over, so he lay face-first on the curb. She raised her foot and curb stomped his head causing his jaw to dislocate, his teeth to fragment into pieces, and his frenzied shrieking to cease. She placed her katana blade in the elbow crease of her jacket sleeve and pulled it through, wiping the blood from the polished steel. She expertly sheathed the blade and made her way back over to the wall of the building. Removing the spray paint can from a pouch on her belt, she shook it causing it to rattle. In bright red paint, she underlined "FUCK OFF." She placed the spray paint can perfectly back into her pouch as she took a deep breath and leaned against the wall once more.

In the run-down bathroom, Grayson discreetly rubbed the serrated trigger of his handgun as he suppressed his conflicted anxiety.

"12-08-29," Carlton desperately stuttered as he shivered in pain and shock.

"Emily's birthday… You sick mother fucker," Grayson muttered under his breath.

"I *loved* her Grayson. I loved her *so much*," Carlton screamed in between pitiful sobs.

"She was a CHILD, Carlton. She was MY child!" Grayson spat in a fury, pounding his chest with his heavy gun.

"I never touched her, Grayson. I swear, I never touched her. I just gave her to them," Carlton began to lose consciousness.

"She was your niece, Carl," said Grayson as a tear slithered through the whiskers on his cheek. He fought to keep his lips from trembling.

"I'm sorry, Grayson. I-,"

BOOM!

Grayson's hand settled from the recoil of the revolver. He lowered the smoking pistol to his side as he looked upon Carlton's pulverized head; eyes bulging from their sockets. Grayson wiped his tears with the sleeve of his leather jacket, holstered his sidearm, and left the bathroom with haste. The swaying and flickering fluorescent light fell from the ceiling and shattered causing the room to go dark.

He emerged from the bathroom door, visibly shaken from Carlton's interrogation. In one hand he clenched the piece of paper with Carlton's name written on it in red ink, in the other he let Emily's bracelet gently hang through his fingers. Faith turned her head to look at him and noticed the sorrow and defeat on his face.

"Hey, you okay, Gray?" She said softly as she hesitantly rested her hand on his shoulder.

"Why did it have to be him?" Grayson asked while fighting the aching lump in his throat.

Faith moved in closer, pressed her body against his, and lightly brushed her thumb against his cheek. She took a breath to prepare a response, but held it in. Instead, she hugged him tightly.

"Did he say why, at least?" Faith inquired while releasing Grayson from her arms.

Grayson unholstered his revolver, opened the cylinder and dumped the empty shells into his bloody hand. He stared at the casings in silence for a moment before transferring them into one of his jacket pockets.

"Why do you think?" Grayson asked rhetorically.

Reading his expression, Faith mimicked injecting a needle into her arm.

Grayson cleared his throat as the impending wave of tears finally subsided.

"Yep," he stated through his held breath.

He reloaded his revolver, re-holstered it under his jacket and let out a calming exhale.

"We'll get her back, Gray," Faith whispered with confidence as her fist clenched the hilt of her katana in a moment of suppressed rage.

"And if we don't..." Grayson started as he looked at his blood-drenched hands, "I won't show them the same mercy I showed my brother."

"Hey, we have to stay focused. Emotion will just get us killed," Faith coldly stated.

"Emotion is the only thing keeping me going, Faith," Grayson retorted. "We should head out before more of these fuckers show up."

Grayson stepped over one of the mangled bodies rotting on the asphalt. Faith sprung over the body and matched pace with Grayson as they disappeared into the darkness of night and headed toward the center of a dingy metropolis with a history so bloody, it was referred to only as Red City by its remaining denizens.

Just as they were turning the corner, a group of skinny children in rags shot out from a nearby alley like little starving coyotes and began looting the bodies.

Chapter 2

Sweet Memories

As Grayson navigated the dark and decrepit streets of the city in silence with Faith, he reflected on the past three years of his life. It was the only way he could drown out the relentless memory of torturing and killing Carlton.

He stared at the crumbling cement moving below his feet as he cursed the cruelty of the universe for placing him, his family, and the entire world in such a dire situation.

Three years ago, an illness was unleashed on the world. The Vola virus seemingly appeared out of nowhere, swiftly wiping out communities worldwide. After it ran rampant for a year and a half, killing millions of people, every major government fell short of developing a vaccine. A cure seemed out of reach as side effects from several prototype vaccines ranged from blindness to heart failure and the mounting pressure from government officials began to weigh heavily on the labs. Several top scientists grew frustrated with bureaucratic red tape delaying a potential vaccine and promptly quit. The private sector was all too eager to employ them.

Within weeks of announcing that they had hired the most prolific scientists and medical experts from around the world, Bio-Yomi came forward with a vaccine. Bio-Yomi was an American medical company backed by the wallet (and interests) of the largest software company in the world.

They were immediately met with heavy criticism from experts since they were only previously known for making impressive breakthroughs in the mechanical prosthetic industry before the Vola virus interrupted the entire world economy. They had no experience developing vaccines, yet they claimed to have been diligently developing it for a year prior to hiring the experts in vaccine development.

Bio-Yomi publicly taunted the U.S. Government, claiming they could end the worldwide sickness and suffering with the prick of a syringe. However, the U.S. Government forbid releasing the vaccine without proper testing and evaluation. Desperation loomed over the United States as world governments and America's citizens threatened violence if the vaccine continued to be blocked by politics and red tape.

Making a power play, Bio-Yomi announced they would be offering the vaccine for free to anyone who came to one of their locations. When the U.S. Government announced they would dispatch the National Guard to shut down the illegal distribution of the vaccine, it sparked an all-out war. Bio-Yomi was met with immediate, unanimous, financial backing from nearly every major world government. Between the private army Bio-Yomi was able to enlist and the desperate, armed populace of America (many of which defected from the military), the National Guard was quickly decimated. Facing missile threats from every armed country in the world and the entire armed populace on the ground, the United States was split in two after the Government submitted.

Half of the United States was run by the Government in an authoritarian fashion with a ban on the vaccine and strict regulations to prevent the spread of the virus. The other half was run by Bio-Yomi, which was completely funded by desperate foreign governments who were purchasing the vaccine.

Most Americans scrambled across the war-torn United States to move to the half of the country with which they agreed. But, as the dust settled and the vaccine was distributed in Bio-Yomi zones of the U.S. and supporting countries, the situation quickly turned disastrous.

Lost in the rhythmic pounding of his own boots, Grayson nibbled the inside of his cheek as he reflected on what would come to be known as Vax Day.

He remembered Faith opening the stained door of their apartment hideout to let a battered Carlton in. As she shut the door, faint gunshots and deep explosions sounded off in the distance.

"I fuckin' got it!" Carlton shouted through his exhausted breath. He wiped the side of his blackened and bleeding face with his shoulder as he held three short syringes in his hand. "One for each of us, baby! Woo!"

Faith walked with purpose to the corner of the disheveled room and retrieved a first aid kit from a military crate.

"You stupid son of a bitch. You actually went," Grayson responded flatly. "The fuck is the matter with you?"

"I'm a slippery little fuck, aren't I?" Carlton proudly stated through a shit-eating grin.

Carlton lightly protested as Faith rolled up the sleeve of his charred shirt and began tending to several burn wounds on his left arm, but gave up and let her continue.

"Well here, take 'em! One for each of ya!" Carlton said through his smile, almost expecting praise.

"I told you not to go, Carl," Grayson said under his breath while nervously massaging his jaw.

"Hey, fuck you Grayson! I'm saving your fucking lives! You didn't have the balls to… Ouch! Goddammit, Faith!"

"Sorry Carl," Faith replied through watery eyes as she sanitized his wound.

Carlton took a breath and calmed his voice.

"You didn't have the balls to go out in that shit-storm to get the vaccine. Like always, I pull through, save your lives, and what do I get? No appreciation, no thank you, no nothing."

"She's pregnant, Carl," Grayson said matter-of-factly.

Faith froze as tears began to collect in her bottom eyelids.

"What did you just say?" Carlton asked, mouth agape.

"She's pregnant."

First, Carlton exhaled in disbelief. He wondered if he heard Grayson correctly. Then his brow furrowed; angered that he had been left out of the loop. Finally, he blew air through closed lips.

"How far-"

"A month," Faith replied with a surprisingly cold delivery as she finished patching up Carlton's arm.

"Well, all the more reason to take the vaccine! You can't afford to get Vola if-"

Faith dropped his sleeve over his freshly gauzed arm, stood up, and looked him square in the eye.

"I'm not putting that shit in my body, Carlton. Don't act like anyone knows what's in that syringe. It's not just me anymore," Faith said sternly. "If I injected that into my body before this shitstorm and it ended up crippling me, I wouldn't give a shit. But I'm not going to risk losing *this* child."

Grayson began anxiously pacing the room.

"Okay, so you don't know what the vaccine could do to you. That's fine, I get that," Carlton responded with his hands in the air. "But you *do* know what Vola will do to you when you catch it. Come on, Grayson! You're on my side here, right? It'll cook your fucking brain and that kid'll ooze out of you looking like an omelet before you die in a pile of your own shit."

Faith grabbed Carlton by the collar of his shirt and twisted it, causing it to choke him. Grayson looked at Faith's other arm and saw the tip of a dagger edging its way down her sleeve.

"Faith!" Grayson firmly shouted.

She looked at Grayson, her eyes darting wildly around the room as she processed her emotions.

"Jesus, I'm sorry, but it's the truth," Carlton managed to choke out. "You've seen it firsthand."

Faith turned her head to face Carlton, headbutted him right in the nose, and pushed him to the floor like discarded trash.

Carlton grunted as he hit the ground holding his bleeding nose.

"Fuck, I'm sorry, okay? It's the fucking truth," he shouted through his cupped hand.

Grayson's fingertips nervously tapped his lips. He wasn't used to feeling this conflicted and out of control.

"So, after all of the bullshit you two have spewed and all of the rebellion shit you've pulled me into," Carlton started has he pushed his way up from the ground onto his feet, "You are going to believe the fucking *Government*. Bio-Yomi says the vaccine is good to go. You're telling me that *you*, Mr. and Mrs. Freedom-Fucking-Fighters, are actually trusting the corrupt-as-hell *Government* that we shouldn't take it?"

"We don't trust anyone, Carl," Grayson assertively responded through tight lips.

"Not even me, Gray?" Carlton genuinely asked as he gripped the syringes tightly.

Carlton removed the cap from a syringe, stuck it in his arm, and depressed the plunger. He tossed the empty syringe into the wall like a dart and held his arms out before letting them drop to his sides.

"If nothing happens to me, you guys are fucking taking yours," Carlton exclaimed while pointing a parental finger at them and moving toward the next room. As he exited into the dark kitchen, he said under his breath, "Cause you're the only fuckin' family I got."

Grayson turned away and ran his fingers through his hair while Faith adjusted the dagger in her sleeve and sighed.

As the thunder of small arms fire died down in the city, Grayson and Faith laid down on a makeshift mattress on the floor of the living area. Surrounded by military supply crates and firearms, Faith's exhaustion took over as she fell asleep immediately while Grayson stared at the ceiling. His mind swirled as he processed the chaos of the city. The unease of literal war echoing through the streets of his home, a deadly virus rampaging across the globe, and the faces of the men whose lives he'd ended in a far-off land coursed through his body like lightning. Tortured by his racing thoughts, the stillness of night finally settled in and sleep took him.

Grayson's eyes violently shot open and he instinctively reached for his handgun beside the mattress. Faith's eyes swiftly opened and she studied Grayson's expression in an attempt to read the situation. The sounds of sobbing traveled through the apartment as a light, rhythmic banging emanated from the kitchen. Grayson stood up from the mattress and slowly neared the source of the crying as Faith followed closely.

As he quietly approached the entryway to the kitchen, Grayson pressed the light switch, revealing Carlton bawling like a desperate child at the table and rhythmically pounding his fist. A damp puddle of tears stained the maps and documents left on the tabletop.

Grayson and Faith noticed two empty syringes resting in front of Carlton's shaking fingertips. Carlton looked up at them and began to lightly beg in between sobs.

"I need more. Grayson. I need more. Grayson. I need more. Grayson."

His voice grew louder as desperation sunk into the pit of his stomach.

"I need *more*. Grayson."

Carlton began aggressively scratching his arms as his face contorted with irritation.

"I need more, Grayson!"

Skin gathered under his fingernails as pink trails formed across his forearms.

"I need more, Grayson!"

Grayson reached out his hand in an attempt to calm his brother.

"It's okay, Carl," Grayson said soothingly.

Carlton's arms began to bleed and his screams turned to shrieks.

"I NEED MORE, GRAYSON!"

Grayson took a soft step forward.

"Hey, Carl. Everything's okay. I'm here."

For a moment, silence washed over the room. Grayson froze as Faith cautiously looked on, letting her blade slip from her sleeve into her hand.

Carlton sat motionless, stared at Grayson and cracked a nervous and shaky smile.

"I need more, Grayson," he quietly pleaded.

Suddenly, the room flashed and turned into a run-down public restroom with flickering fluorescent lights. Grayson watched as Carlton's head violently exploded into a pulp, leaving behind a deflated, bloody face. Carlton's body fell between two urinals and Grayson looked down at his own hand that wielded a smoking revolver.

Chapter 3

BEHEMOTH

"I'm sorry, Carlton," Grayson said aloud through trembling lips as he was jolted back to reality from his haunting memories.

"Gray, keep it together. We're almost there," Faith replied with a worried expression as they crossed an abandoned city street lined with burned cars and crumbling remains of buildings. A helicopter roared through the night sky overhead in the direction of a well-lit, towering glass building. Sweeping rooftop spotlights lit up the sky above the building and beckoned the approaching chopper. At the top of the building read "Bio-Yomi" in bright, white letters and above it sat a neon-red logo of an arch reminiscent of Torii gate.

"All of that fighting and not so much as a smudge on a single window in that place," Grayson mentioned as they approached the intersection at the end of the street.

"Well, they had one hell of an army," Faith responded.

Grayson surveyed his surroundings and casually said, "Yeah, so did we."

Faith noticed a man hiding in a beat-up car, seemingly lying in wait. She motioned his location to Grayson.

She chuckled and said, "The Government had the best army and look how that turned out for them."

"They were fighting us, too, though," Grayson replied. "By the time we figured out Bio-Yomi were pieces of shit, there weren't enough of us left to stand a chance."

"Nothing to gain from fighting them either," Faith added. "Come on, let's get this over with."

"We're nearly there. Let's not fuck it up now," Grayson responded as he scanned the barren rooftops and broken windows of the surrounding buildings.

Faith dropped her slight smirk, took a breath, and walked toward the car with the man in it. The *clip-clop* of her leather boots echoed down the empty street as her eyes darted side to side looking for more potential threats. As she neared the vehicle, she pushed her katana an inch out of its sheath with her thumb.

"Come on out, douche bag!" Faith hollered.

A short and dirty man in rags frantically scrambled through the rear window of the rusted car and stood hunched over in front of Faith.

"I- I- I- I didn't mean nothin'! Wasn't tryin' to scramble ya- er, scare ya!" He twitched and shook his head as he tried to correct his grammar as he spoke.

Faith, cool and calm, shifted her weight and confidently placed her hand on the grip of her sword.

"Do you have any other creepy friends hanging around here waiting to *scramble* me?"

"I- I- didn't mean to say s-scramble!" He yelled while nervously scratching various parts of his body. His eyes widened and his jaw dropped in horror. "Oh- Oh no! You- you're Faith!"

The tight clicking of a revolver cocking interrupted the man's thought process as Grayson, who had flanked the man, leveled the barrel of his hand cannon at the back of his head from a few arms-lengths away.

"Then that must make me Grayson," he said as the man's knees began to waver.

"I'm glad you've heard of us," Faith commented. She let the blade of her sword fall completely back into its scabbard with a "*click.*" "What's the bounty up to now?"

"Th-th-three," the man shakily responded with his hands up in the air.

"Crates? Jesus, they want us bad," Grayson exclaimed from behind his gun.

"Y-y-yeah, three crates of Vax. Do *you* guys have any on ya?" the man asked as his head ticked and bobbed like a hungry bird.

"Any idea what the Government bounty is," Faith asked out of curiosity.

"A million, l-last time I heard."

"Eh, still not enough to motivate anyone to cross zones for us," Grayson said.

"N- n- no one's gonna believe I saw ya guys! Y- yer like celebrities! With all the damage you d-d-did to the

Government… And then t- to Bio-Yomi after Vax Day. Shit, I'd like y-y-yer autographs!"

"Come on, Grayson. Time to go. It's just a few more corners 'till we're there," Faith said with an exhausted undertone. She turned around, began walking down the street and motioned for Grayson to follow with her gloved hand.

Grayson de-cocked his revolver by thumbing the hammer down and lowered the muzzle away from the man's head.

"F-fer real, though," the man began. "If ya f-find any Vax, you'll let me k-know?" The man asked as he turned to face Grayson.

As the man completed his turn, Grayson watched him freeze. The man's breath was shallow as he appeared to be paralyzed with fear.

"What, never seen a little blood before?" Grayson asked as he motioned to the dried blood on his clothing.

Then Grayson froze, his head slightly turned as he listened closely.

Thud.

Thud.

Thud. Thud. Thud.

As Grayson pinpointed the source of the sound, he turned around and faced the dark alley behind him. A seven-foot-tall, hulking figure sprinted toward him.

Grayson ducked as a haymaker punch rocketed over his head.

Faith whipped around as a blood curdling scream emanated from the ragged man. Her eyes focused on his hunched body that was now levitating three-feet off the ground. A blood-dripping fist protruded from the man's back as the gigantic figure lifted him up, impaled on his arm. The man's screams devolved into gurgles as the figure tossed the blood-gargling corpse across the street and shook the blood off its arm with a thick *splat.*

Without hesitation, Faith ran toward the gargantuan figure with her hand gripping her sheathed katana. However, since she had walked halfway down the street, she had significant ground to cover.

Meanwhile, Grayson hastily scrambled to his feet after dodging the thunderous punch. The giant figure, after discarding his unintended victim, slowly turned to face him down.

Grayson's eyes focused on the figure's bulky and bloody right arm. Steel reinforced tubing and wires weaved in and out of the muscular limb. A smooth, hydraulic piston was fused to the outside of its hefty forearm. On its huge hand rested a thick, rectangular section of steel, adorned with metallic and aggressive looking knuckles attached to a smaller piston-driven system. It's boulder-like bicep was completely encased in flexible steel and gently pulsed as the grinding and whirring of mechanical parts hummed from within.

As Grayson glanced up to comprehend what he was looking at, he saw that attached to the massive mechanical arm was a seven-foot-tall, bald, colossal man wearing a carbon-fiber patterned poncho that covered everything but his head and right arm. Fused to his forehead was metal plating that continued down and surrounded a white, robotic eye on the right side of his face. A large, metallic jaw rounded off the bottom of the man's head while the rest of his face was covered in weathered skin. Steel teeth lined his jaw and upper gums. Grayson let out an involuntary gasp as he noticed the teeth were particularly accentuated by the man's lack of lips. The left, noticeably human eye in the man's skull stared down at Grayson with a fuming hatred.

Grayson deftly raised his revolver and pulled the double action trigger. The cylinder rotated and the hammer cycled, igniting a vicious blast from the muzzle of the gun. The man's poncho violently ripped where the .44 magnum bullet entered, but he seemed unaffected as the bullet exited his back with great velocity.

The man's metallic jaw opened and out came a synthesized groan. Grayson continued to fire three more concussive blasts at the man as he backed himself into a brick wall. Two bullets entered and exited the man's chest with great force and one bullet ricocheted off his head, causing his human eye to angrily squint. The airy groan turned to a primal growl as the man, with surprising speed, cocked his arm for a punch and swung with deadly precision toward Grayson's face.

"Grayson, no!" Faith desperately screamed, only a few strides away.

With a taxed grimace, Grayson stumbled to the side, narrowly avoided the punch, and fell backward onto the rough sidewalk. The sheer force of the punch blew Grayson's leather jacket back as it connected with the brick wall behind him. The man's powerful arm penetrated the wall up to his elbow and sent spiderweb patterned cracks up to the roof of the building and down the sidewalk toward Grayson.

Grayson's eyes widened as he realized the hydraulic pistons did not even activate and remained stationary through the punch. The gargantuan man placed his other, seemingly organic, hand on the wall and began to remove his arm from the side of the building.

Faith closed in on the man's rear, drew her katana, and thrust it toward the man's lower back. The man's head turned and the robotic eye noticed the strike in his peripheral vision. A two-foot-long spike instantly extended from behind his elbow, striking the blade of Faith's sword.

Her katana was ripped from her hands and flew twenty-five yards before piercing the trunk of a burnt car down the street where it stuck upright and vibrated from tip to handle. Without hesitation, she punched her arm out to the side and caught the handle of her dagger as it exited her sleeve. In a single agile motion, she plunged the dagger into the man's back. The knife was sucked out of her hand into the man's poncho which began to flap violently as if a tornado were underneath it. Faith inspected her empty hands in confusion.

Grayson had pushed himself off the ground, cocked the hammer of his revolver, and paused to aim precisely at the man's human eye.

As Grayson lined up his sights, the man let out vibrating grumble through his metal teeth.

"*Grayyyyysssonnn.*"

Suddenly, Faiths dagger shot out from the front of the man's poncho like a bullet. It impacted Grayson's leg, pierced deep into his shinbone, and swept him clean off his feet. As he impacted the ground, his firearm discharged into the sidewalk sending chunks of concrete flying.

"Gray!" Faith shouted as her eyes fought off a wave of helpless tears.

Grayson, with the adrenaline rush of a wounded animal, pushed himself off the ground.

"Faith, run!" He shouted as he took three painful strides away from the indestructible behemoth. He had to do a double-take over his shoulder as he watched Faith running in the wrong direction.

"Goddammit! Over here!" he yelled through gritted teeth while motioning for her to follow with his gun in hand.

The towering man observed Grayson's concern for Faith.

"Dad's sword!" was all she yelled back.

The man opened his jaw and let out a wispy grunt of superiority as he turned to follow Faith.

"Fuck! Faith, leave it!" Grayson shouted.

Knowing she would never leave her father's sword behind; Grayson ran after the man while ignoring the pain searing through his leg.

The behemoth's heavy footsteps picked up pace behind Faith as Grayson jumped on the hood of the car the ragged man previously hid in. He cocked the hammer of his revolver once more, lined up his sights and tracked the man's head. With his target moving laterally at twenty yards, Grayson exhaled and squeezed the trigger. The second the hammer began to fall, Grayson winced. He knew he had missed.

Faith slammed into the back of the car and grabbed the hilt of her sword that was sticking straight out of the abandoned vehicle's trunk. Her moment of relief turned to despair as she turned and saw the rushing behemoth cocking his mechanical arm back.

Boom!

Grayson's shot echoed down the street. The bullet landed with a dull, wet impact as it struck the man's normal hand. The ring and pinky fingers exploded off of the hand like missiles as a torrent of dark blood fell from the shredded skin.

A nightmarish, electrical scream filled the night sky as the man dropped his mechanical arm to his side and raised his bleeding hand to his face. His organic eye bulged with rage and anguish as he stared at his wounded hand, in shock.

Faith ripped the sword from the trunk and dashed toward Grayson who was begging her to move faster.

"Let's go!" Grayson screamed, still atop the hood of the car.

All Faith could muster were winded whimpers as a tear streamed around her face and into her hair. She finally reached Grayson who used her as a brace to step down from the car. The knife deep in his shin was finally starting to overwhelm him.

"You're okay, you're okay," he reassured Faith.

"I know," she defiantly replied while wiping the trail of her single tear with the sleeve of her jacket. "Good shot," she mentioned.

"All skill," he replied as she finished helping him down from the car.

They both looked over at the man who was now hunched over his bleeding hand. His head snapped over in their direction as his robotic eye twisted and focused on them.

"Maybe we should try talking to him," Grayson suggested jokingly.

Another nightmarish scream shook the ground as the man's feet pushed off of the asphalt causing it to crush and crumble underneath him.

"Time to go, Gray!" Faith called out as they turned to flee.

"I'm trying! Your knife is in my fucking leg!"

Thud. Thud. Thud.

The behemoth let out another earsplitting scream as it ran toward them with his bleeding arm dangling like a ragdoll behind him.

"Now!" Faith yelled as she grabbed Grayson's jacket and pulled him away from the car.

Fatigued and in pain, they frantically tried not to trip over themselves as they dashed away. With a decent head start, they were quickly nearing the upcoming intersection.

The behemoth, realizing they were nearly out of reach, cocked his arm back in a blind rampage as he sprinted toward the car they had just retreated from. His growl grew in intensity as the piston in his arm compressed and locked into place. He then closed all five of his steel fingers, each one clanking against his palm as he balled his fist and the piston in his knuckles compressed.

Thud. Thud. Thud.

His growl turned into a deep battle cry as his bicep grew red hot and the flexible steel swelled up, inflating with energy.

Thud. Thud. Thud.

Reacting to the ear-splitting sound of the battle cry, Faith and Grayson looked over their shoulders as the behemoth reached the car they had just retreated from.

From an all-out sprint, the behemoth released his punch. His fist landed square in the grill of the car as both pistons in his arm violently released and extended, crunching the vehicle's front end. A powerful shockwave burst through the car as the metal crumpled and wrinkled across the vehicle's body. The asphalt underneath began to explode as if it were being carpet bombed and a blinding flash of light ripped through the car. All at once, the vehicle exploded into a wall of shrapnel as a visible wave of energy launched from the behemoth's arm. Several metallic flaps opened from the flexible steel in his bicep to vent out scorching blue flames and high-pressure steam.

The rear bumper of the vehicle rocketed towards Grayson. Faith reflexively slashed upward with her katana, slicing it in two. The two halves split and shot around them as thousands of pieces of shrapnel hurtled toward them as if they were fired from a rail gun. Grayson grabbed Faith around her waist and jumped around the corner of the street, falling behind the cover of the building. A lightning-fast tornado of shrapnel careened past them as the ground began to rumble and shake.

Panicked, Grayson and Faith fought their way to their feet and sprinted like hell. As they crossed the street, Grayson glanced over his shoulder and witnessed the road splitting in two and separating as if a sinkhole were forming

"We're almost there! Left here!" Faith commanded.

They turned down an alleyway, leaving behind the carnage the behemoth had wrought.

The flaps folded back down onto the behemoth's bicep as the pistons returned to their neutral positions. Spiritually crushed by his victims' escape, his human eye began to dart around as he came to terms with his failure. The buildings around him began to collapse and, just as he was swallowed by a cloud of dust, he let out a final rage-induced roar that echoed through the entire city.

CHAPTER 4
HOME AGAIN

"Have you ever seen anything like that before?" Grayson grumbled as he hobbled down an alleyway riddled with empty Bio-Yomi vaccine cases. He was gripping his pants at thigh-level helping his injured leg move along.

"Yeah, I've seen that *hundreds* of times. Just forgot to mention it," Faith replied as she walked a few paces ahead of him, scanning the area as they advanced.

"I mean, the *arm* on that thing... That fucker had to be Bio-Yomi, right? For real, did you ever see anything like that when your dad was there?"

Faith gripped the handle of her sheathed sword and ran her thumb across it.

"No, Bio-Yomi just made advanced prosthetics when my dad was there. Not… whatever *that* was. But, if anyone outside of Bio-Yomi knows anything about… *that*… It'll be Kurt," Faith responded. "Speaking of Kurt, we're here."

They came to a stop about fifty feet from a large garage door at the end of the alley. Faith looked up at a security camera that was mounted on the alleyway wall and waved at it. Grayson took the weight off of his injured leg, leaned against the wall, and gave a half-hearted wave.

Underneath the camera was an intercom speaker and red graffiti artwork of a crow's head encircled by barbed wire. A portion of the barbed wire had worn away, so Faith removed her spray paint can from its pouch. With a few quick sprays, she had touched it up to perfection.

After a few seconds, the intercom under the camera emitted a raspy voice.

"You're good," the voice crackled.

Faith gave the camera a thumbs up and began to move forward. Grayson, however, winced as he put some weight on his leg that still had a knife handle sticking out of it.

"Need some help there?" Faith asked while smirking.

"Adrenaline's gone, definitely starting to feel it," Grayson replied as he limped forward.

As they progressed down the alleyway, they passed a dozen claymore mines placed at varying heights all rigged to motion sensors.

"I thought it had me," Faith said under her breath.

Grayson, hobbling, looked at her inquisitively.

"When I was getting my dad's sword…" she continued as she fought to keep her voice from shaking. "In that moment, I thought I had failed Emily. If I die, the chances of finding her… She needs her mom, Gray."

As they reached the garage door, it slowly opened for them.

"I know, and I wasn't about to let that happen," Grayson said reassuringly.

"I let my emotions get the better of me, I just couldn't leave Dad's sword-"

Grayson placed his rough hand on her shoulder, causing her to stop.

"Listen, emotion is the only thing keeping me going. Whatever the fuck that thing was out there isn't going to stop me from getting our daughter back. What did your *dad* used to say about emotion?"

The garage door reached the top and the building awaited their entry.

"Let's go," Faith said flatly as she walked inside.

"Hey, wait!" Grayson hollered. "Fuck, ow," he grunted as he hobbled into the building and the garage door lowered behind him.

The lights flickered on in a large workshop filled with various gadgets and tools. Bio-Yomi logos crossed out with red spray paint adorned the walls.

"Holy shit! Where in the fuck did he find this?" Grayson exclaimed with an awe-inspired smile strewn across his face.

In the center of the workshop sat a black pickup truck retrofitted with bolted-on armor. In the bed was a mounted .50 caliber Browning belt-fed machine gun.

"I traded a Vax smuggler a map of underground routes into a few Government zones," Kurt said with a gruff, but upbeat voice from the top of the staircase that led to the interior.

They looked up at Kurt, a burly elderly man with a bald head and a thinning white beard. He wore an olive-green apron covered in grease and he stood on two carbon fiber prosthetic legs.

"Did it come with gas?" Grayson inquired.

"Full tank!" Kurt proudly answered.

"Well, shit. That alone was a fair trade!" Grayson replied, patting the armored hood of the truck.

Faith made her way toward the staircase as Grayson quickly limped to catch up.

"Glad you both made it back safe! Sounded like a damn H-Bomb was dropped down the street! The hell *was* that?" Kurt asked as his grimy fingers wrapped around the railing of the staircase.

Faith quietly walked past him, patted him on the shoulder and entered the interior of the building.

Grayson slowly worked his way up the staircase one step at a time as he used the railing for support.

"You got a knife stuck in your shin," Kurt pointed out.

Grayson managed to release a tired chuckle through the pain.

"At least I have a shin, old man," Grayson clapped back.

"Hey, joke about my legs all you want. But you cut that 'old man' shit out," Kurt responded with a faux stern face and a pointed finger.

Grayson finally reached Kurt, who was now holding the door open at the top of the stairs for him. Grayson paused in the doorway.

"We need to talk," Grayson said as he observed Kurt's jocund expression. "This is serious shit, Kurt. We *really* need to talk."

Kurt's smile fell and he put his hand on the back of Grayson's jacket.

"Let's talk while I look at that leg of yours. Did Faith go to her studio?" Kurt asked as he led Grayson inside.

"That'd be my guess. She got pretty shook up out there."

Kurt and Grayson walked into a large main room with tools, storage cases, and carbon fiber prosthetics scattered about. Five branching paths surrounded the white-tiled entryway, each leading to different wings of the building. It had no windows or skylights and was akin to a hidden fortress.

"Faith? Shook up? Did you find Carlton?" Kurt began questioning.

Grayson instantly pictured Carlton's head, popped like a zit, in a grungy bathroom. He could smell the gunpowder and his eye twitched at the invasive memory.

"Just sit me down and I'll explain everything. This thing's fucking killing me."

Kurt guided Grayson into a makeshift hospital room with dusty medical devices and monitors. Grayson plopped down on a stained bed with a vocal sigh of relief as Kurt shuffled a chair toward him.

"Up!" Kurt shouted as he scooted the chair.

Grayson, cupping his leg with both hands, lifted his foot up and rested it on the seat.

Kurt grabbed a pair of medical shears and cut Grayson's pant leg up to the wound to get a better look. He then grabbed the handle of the knife with three fingers and wiggled it.

Grayson let out a yelp and Kurt released the handle.

"Well, that's right in the bone," Kurt observed.

"I could've told you that! You didn't have to jerk it around!" Grayson angrily stated.

"I didn't jerk it around; it was just a wiggle," Kurt said, prodding him on.

"I've been stabbed before, but never in the fucking bone. So, how in the hell do we do this? It's *really* in there," Grayson reminded him through sharp inhales of pain.

"Well, I've got a prosthetic that'll fit you perfectly," Kurt started to say.

"Enough with the jokes, what can we do about it?"

"Well, I can tell you what *I* can do about it. Which is, essentially, grinding down the bone on either side of the blade until it falls out. If you think it hurts while it's in you,

you'll leave this room with a whole new pain tolerance once it's out of you," Kurt informed him.

"Is there... another option?" Grayson asked reluctantly.

"We leave it in," Kurt stated plainly.

"Can I think about it?" Grayson asked through a nervous chuckle.

Kurt walked to the corner of the room and retrieved a wheelchair.

"Sure! Here, hop in and we'll head to the kitchen so you can catch me up on current events over some coffee," Kurt replied impatiently.

Grayson painfully scooted himself into the wheelchair. Kurt propped one of the pedals up, so Grayson's leg could stay elevated.

"Grab the safe and bring it into the kitchen. If what you said is true, whatever's in that safe will lead us to Emily. And we don't have any fucking time to lose," Grayson stated in a hurry.

Kurt started pushing him in the wheelchair, his prosthetic limbs mechanically creaking as he walked.

"I'm an information broker, Grayson. Just because I've been housing you guys, doesn't mean you get anything for free around here," Kurt explained matter-of-factly.

"Enough, Kurt. Emily is out there in that fucking city all alone," Grayson snapped.

"All right, all right, I'll grab the safe. But we aren't opening it until you tell me everything that happened. I'm assuming you found the code?"

Grayson sighed and turned his head slightly.

"Yeah, I got the code."

Kurt pushed Grayson into the large entryway and down a different hallway toward the kitchen.

Meanwhile, Faith closed the door to her studio, removed her sheathed katana from her belt, leaned against the door, and slid down to a seated position on the floor. She quietly sobbed while hugging her sword.

Her studio was covered wall-to-wall in graffiti-style street art. One half of the room was littered with spray paint cans, stencils, and supplies while the other half sat perfectly neat and organized with kendo gear. Two sets of bamboo swords, two sets of wooden swords, and two sets of kendo armor were mounted on the wall in pairs.

Faith slowed her heaving chest, tamed her sobs, and managed to catch her breath. She shuffled to her knees, sat on her heels, and rested her hands in her lap. Her tight muscles began to loosen and she cleared her throat before letting out a powerful exhale.

"Feeling emotion does not make you weak. Failing to *control* emotion does," Faith recited.

She rose to her feet and walked over to an antique desk sitting in the back of the room. The old wooden office chair creaked as she sat in it and leaned forward, resting her katana against the side of the desk. She moved two large, rectangular whetstones to the corner of the desk before picking up and unplugging a charging smartphone with a cracked screen. The corner of the display showed a full battery, but no service.

Faith brushed her hair out of her face and took in a deep breath before tapping on the 'photos' icon. Her hand gently trembled as she cycled through photos of Emily featuring Faith, Grayson, and Kurt. The most recent photos consisted of pictures of an adorable two-year-old Emily, which then regressed to a baby Emily, followed by photos of Grayson and Faith traveling together with much younger faces. She couldn't help but crack a smile at the thought of life before the rebellion. Faith then scrolled to family photos prominently featuring herself and her father at her national and international kendo championship matches.

"I miss you, Dad," Faith whispered with a glum tone.

As Faith scrolled quickly through the photos, she suddenly froze. Her finger hovered over the screen for a moment before she slowly moved it out of the way revealing a gorgeous, smiling, pregnant woman sitting in front of a nearly finished canvas painting holding a pallet and several brushes. The painting consisted of a stylistic cherry blossom tree and above it read 'Have Faith.' Faith wiped one final tear that lazily swam down her cheek.

She turned the smartphone off, pushed herself away from the desk, and grabbed her katana, sliding it into her belt. With a purposeful stride, she exited her studio in search of Grayson and Kurt.

Faith peered into the messy kitchen to see Grayson in a wheelchair with his knifed-leg elevated as he sipped on a cup of coffee. Kurt leaned against stacked carbon-fiber Bio-Yomi crates while cradling his own cup.

"I'm really sorry about your brother, Grayson. I was really hoping he'd come back peacefully with you," Kurt said consolingly as he stared into his cup.

"He was… Too far gone. I guess the Vax addiction fried his brain because he didn't just *think* he was protecting us by taking Emily. He *knew* it. And we ended up finding him on the street with two briefcases full of Vax. I'm not sure if he was hoarding it or selling it, but it must have been payment for Emily," Grayson explained.

Faith looked on as Kurt's eyes sorrowfully stared into space and his thumb caressed his coffee cup.

"I- I'm sorry he got away with Emily, Grayson. If only I would have kept an eye…" Kurt explained, his voice wavering.

"Hey, I let him in here, Kurt. This is on me," Grayson said, avoiding eye contact with Kurt. "You knew he was lying the second you saw him, didn't you?"

"He may have been your brother, but I'll be damned if he doesn't… *didn't*… walk, talk, and act like a snake."

Faith stepped into the doorway of the kitchen, making her presence known. Kurt quickly shed the worry from his face and cleared his throat.

"Faith! You feelin' better, darlin'?" Kurt quipped.

"Did Gray tell you everything?" Faith quickly asked, deflecting the question.

Faith walked up behind Grayson and placed her hand on his shoulder. He slid his hand over hers and gripped it gently.

"Yep, and it sure as hell explains the nuke that went off around the corner. And I'll be damned if that isn't Bio-Yomi tech. Faith, right around the time your father and I left the company, they were working on weaponizing prosthetics using the biomagnetic energy source we developed. That creepy Borka bastard headed up the repurposing initiative for our energy source. That's the whole damned reason they snatched up those experts and developed the vaccine. There are no wars to fight if everyone's dropping like moths in a fire from the Vola Virus. No war means no need for weapons. No need for weapons, means Bio-Yomi dumped their entire budget in the trash. It was sink or swim, so they decided to sink the whole world so they could swim."

All worked up from his tirade, Kurt sipped from an empty cup, grumbled, and set it down on a crate before crossing his arms.

"Like I said before, Bio-Yomi has our daughter," Faith stated, removing her hand from Grayson's shoulder.

"Other than your 'motherly intuition' you don't know that," Grayson responded. "Does Bio-Yomi have a bone to pick with us? Of course. We royally fucked them. But why go through the trouble to pay off my brother to take Emily? Why not just send that creature to kill us, like they clearly did? It just doesn't make sense."

Kurt uncrossed his arms and began moving Bio-Yomi crates aside.

"All right you two, stop your damn whining. You're giving me flashbacks of my last marriage," Kurt yelled before pausing for a moment. "Although, these days it'd be worth having that ol' hag around for just a night..." Kurt chuckled in an attempt to pass it off as a joke.

He pushed aside the final crate revealing a small, but sturdy, rectangular safe with a keypad.

"I'd say you two have given me enough juicy gossip to afford this sucker, which, by the way, cost me an arm and a leg to acquire. I give you one safe obtained from Carlton's hideout. I'd have cracked it for you, but like I said... This little son of a gun is rigged to blow. And while I've grown accustomed to my prosthetic legs, I'm still quite attached to my hands. Especially living a womanless life..."

Grayson waved his hand in front of his face in an attempt to erase the visualization forced upon him as Faith rolled her eyes and shifted her weight.

"Spare us, Kurt," Grayson muttered in disgust. "Faith, you're up."

Faith approached the safe and squatted in front of it. She calmed her hand that trembled ever so slightly.

"Ready," Faith informed Grayson.

"It's… Emily's birthday. Twelve, zero, eight, two, nine," Grayson stated as his voice trailed off.

Kurt closed his eyes in revulsion as Faith controlled the raging demon inside her.

As Grayson recited the code, he looked down and saw a newborn Emily in his arms, still wrapped in a towel. Suddenly, he was laying on his back in a patch of grass. A ten-year-old Carlton stood over him and reached his hand out.

"Come on, Grayson, get up!" Carlton shouted with a childlike voice before a gunshot rang out and a bullet ripped through his face.

Grayson looked around and noticed he was surrounded by soldiers. Bullets whistled past him as a cruise missile rocketed overhead. An explosion muted his hearing as a child's severed arm landed at his feet and a wave of dirt rushed toward him.

He blinked and when he opened his eyes, he was looking through the crosshairs of a scoped rifle tracking a sprinting civilian holding a Bio-Yomi case on a dark city street.

"Goddammit, put it down. Don't make me…" Grayson said to himself as he slowly squeezed the trigger.

"Grayson!" Faith shouted.

Grayson blinked and saw Faith crouching in front of the open safe looking back at him. He flinched when he realized Kurt was shaking his shoulder.

"Gray, you're not there, baby," Faith said firmly. "It's okay, you're here now. Pull it together for Emily."

Grayson noticed that his heart was beating faster than he could hear it and his clothes were drenched with sweat. Kurt patted him on the chest and wheeled him closer to the safe as he breathed deeply.

"I'm sorry..."

"Don't you say another word, now," Kurt said, calmly interrupting him.

Grayson's chest rose and fell as the color came back to his face.

"What do we have?" Grayson asked, finally regaining his bearings.

Faith stood up, walked closer to Grayson, and held out her hands. In her left hand rested a smart phone, and in her right hand was a plain-looking notebook with a carbon-fiber patterned cover.

"Anything else?" Grayson asked, a little underwhelmed.

Kurt crouched down and began scooping syringes out of the safe into a foam-padded container.

"Just a shit-ton of Vax," Kurt responded casually.

Faith tossed the notebook into Grayson's lap and sat in a nearby chair, leaning forward, and bringing the smartphone closer to her eyes.

Grayson flipped through the notebook page-by-page, skimming through meet times, syringe counts, and aliases. Finally, he reached a page titled 'Project SF.' Unlike the other pages, this one had an entire paragraph scribbled across it.

"I think I've got something, listen to this," Grayson declared, his heartbeat quickening. "Spoke to K.N. today. Told her they trust me now. We are on. Gotta do the unspeakable, but Grayson gets to live and I get a lifetime supply. I've only lived with 'em for a week, but that little squirt has grown on me more than I could have imagined. I've wanted to meet her for so long. I feel physical pain just thinking about doing it. This'll be harder than I thought. But I promised Mom and Dad I'd keep him safe. The years may pass, but my promise lasts forever. I'm not about to stop now," Grayson recited from the notebook.

He took a few moments to process what he read before flipping through the remaining blank pages.

"After that, it's empty."

"K.N.," Kurt repeated as he set down his new case of Vax. "Lifetime supply? Did you all land on the same K.N. I just did?"

"Anything on the phone?" Grayson hurriedly asked Faith.

"The phone is empty," Faith responded. "But it actually has service and there is a single contact listed: K.N."

Faith turned the phone in her hand to show Grayson and Kurt the contact list and the full bars of cell service. Kurt rubbed his eyebrows and sighed.

"Bio-Yomi employees are the only ones with access to the cell towers, and unless you can think of another Bio-Yomi employee with the initials K.N.," Kurt deduced while placing his hands on his hips, "Then, we're in shit deeper than we can breathe in. And it sure explains that multi-billion-dollar walking warhead they sent your way."

Faith stared at the screen for a moment as Kurt spoke. She then took a leap of faith and initiated a call with the contact named 'K.N.'

"Faith... What are you doing?" A stunned Grayson asked.

"I'm getting our daughter back," Faith responded with a gaze of determination.

Chapter 5
Figurehead

Dr. Gaspar Borka straightened the I.D. card on his white lab coat and scratched the dark five o'clock shadow on his pitted face with his long, bony fingers. His untrimmed fingernails scratched his nose as he checked his breath against his hand and cleared his throat. He stood in front of frosted, double sliding doors in a bleach-white hallway as a scummy looking man in a straitjacket, who was strapped to a dolly, whimpered through a white muzzle. Above the doors was a blue, hologram name plate that read: Chief Operating Officer – Kimberly Naito.

"Shut up, swine," Borka nastily ordered while kicking the dolly with a *clang*.

Borka reached out and pressed his barcoded wrist band against a scanner next to the door. The scanner beeped in confirmation.

"How may I help you?" An artificial voice inquired.

"Doctor Borka for Ms. Naito," Borka responded through a yellowing, Cheshire grin.

"Thank you, Doctor Borka. You may enter," the artificial voice said welcomingly.

The frosted doors turned crystal-clear and parted, revealing a ridiculously large office outfitted from the floor to the ceiling in polished white, marble tile. The size of the room was truly staggering, causing Borka's footsteps and one of the dolly's squeaky wheels to resound across the blank, seamless walls. The only furniture in the room was a spacious, glass desk at the back of the room, behind which, sat a petite woman in her mid-thirties sporting a white, designer blazer with a matching skirt and nude heels.

As Borka arrived at the center of the room, he subtly bowed. The woman behind the desk leaned back in her white, leather chair and crossed her bronzed legs.

"Ms. Naito, today I have…" Borka began to recite.

"Is this going to be messy, Borka?" Ms. Naito said unexcitedly, interrupting Borka's pitch.

"Y- Yes, Ms. Naito," Borka stammered.

The man strapped to the dolly began to scream through his muzzle once again as his eyes darted around the room. Ms. Naito touched her glass desk and a blue hologram of a keyboard appeared. Her long, red fingernail tapped a command key and a slot opened in the floor around her desk. A clear, nine-foot-tall shield raised from the slot in the blink of an eye, surrounding the front and sides of her desk.

"You have one minute," Ms. Naito informed Borka.

"Yes, Ms. Naito!" Borka barked, subtly bowing again.

As Borka undid the straps on the dolly, he recited his pitch like a showy magician.

"Ms. Naito, today I have for you, the future of military medical equipment."

Ms. Naito crossed her arms and sighed, completely disinterested.

The man in the straight-jacket fell from the dolly and landed on his face with a *thud.*

"Stand up, you little bastard," Borka frustratingly muttered to the man as he attempted to lift him to his feet. "You are making me *look bad.*"

Borka managed to bring the man up to his feet and leaned intimately close to the man's ear.

"Stand still, or I'll finish what I started in the lab," Borka whispered to the man.

The man's white pants creased as he clenched his buttocks together and quietly sobbed.

Borka retrieved a carbon-fiber prosthetic leg, a miniature device resembling a hockey puck, and a remote switch from the back of the dolly. He peeled a sticky backing off of the puck and slapped it onto the man's knee.

"Let's say you are on the battlefield and your fellow soldier is grievously injured, resulting in loss of limb," Borka spoke hypothetically. "This is where the Field Prosthetic comes into play."

Borka took a few steps back, leaned away from the man and pressed the remote switch. The puck attached to the man's leg detonated causing a controlled explosion to rip through his limb, detaching it below the knee. Ms. Naito blinked as a few speckles of blood and bone hit her shield with force. The man's calf slid across the floor as he collapsed onto his back while screaming through muffled gasps of air. He lifted what was left of his leg and stared at it with wide eyes while writhing around in his straitjacket. Blood fell from the limb in great volumes, pooling on the stark-white floor.

"Normally you would have to sacrifice two able-bodied soldiers to evacuate the wounded. But now, with the Field Prosthetic, you can get the wounded soldier back in the fight!" Borka yelled over the man's panicked yelps.

Borka approached the man, grabbed his thigh, and slowly moved the prosthetic closer to the wound. Suddenly, a long, spiked screw shot out from the prosthetic and stabbed into the bloody stump. Borka released the prosthetic as it screwed itself into the man's leg. The man began to choke through intense pain.

"And voila! The soldier is ready to fight once again! Rise, soldier and continue the battle!" Borka valiantly commanded.

The man scurried to his knees and as he placed weight on the limb he vomited into his muzzle from the pain and released a gargling shriek.

"I… I said, rise soldier! And continue the battle!"

Ms. Naito hit another command key on her desk, causing a slot to open in the ceiling above her desk. A heavy machine gun turret lowered and, as she hit another key, it locked onto the man's head and fired.

The man's head cracked in half like an egg and his brains spilled out like a chunky yolk. His screams were instantly silenced.

"Borka, I want things that cause damage, not fix damage. There's no money in fixing damage unless you can cause it first." Ms. Naito angrily nagged. "And for fuck's sake, Borka, you can't fight when you are in that much pain, you didn't even think this through. I'm growing impatient with your recent disappointments. You should be working on the setbacks with Project Steel Fist, not experimenting with this nonsense. I need Izanami up and running by the end of the quarter and until you sort out the *issue* with Steel Fist, I'm not going anywhere near that death trap of a suit."

"I cannot proceed with Project Steel Fist until the team recovers him from the field and he is recharged to full capacity. As far as your Izanami project goes… well, you see, the little girl…" Borka whined before Ms. Naito cut him off.

"No more stalling with the girl. You are either going to do it or…"

A light, rhythmic vibration sounded off near Ms. Naito's desk. She stopped mid-sentence, tapped another command key, and a miniature tower filled with smartphones elevated from a slot in the floor. As she scanned the tower, she noticed a phone in the middle of the tower with a lit-up screen. She grabbed it and noticed the contact that initiated the call was named "CA."

"Leave now," Ms. Naito commanded in a raised tone.

"But, Ms. N…" Borka started to say with a worried expression.

Ms. Naito tapped a command key on her desk and the turret locked on to Borka.

"Now," Ms. Naito said shortly.

Borka turned tail and ran from the room. With the press of another command key on her desk, Ms. Naito closed her office doors causing them to return to their frosted state.

She stared at the incoming call for a few seconds as she played a mental chess game, attempting to anticipate the impending conversation. Feeling confident, she whipped her hair to one side, answered the call, and placed the phone to her ear.

"Carlton, my dear, I wasn't expecting a call from beyond the grave. Unless this is… Grayson?" Ms. Naito asked with a self-satisfied smile across her face.

"Listen up, bitch. I'm going to give you one chance to give me my daughter back or I will come over there and send that entire building crashing to the ground," Faith's voice firmly stated over the phone.

"You amuse me… Faith? Is it? If you think you can tell me what to do, then you clearly have no idea with whom you are speaking," Ms. Naito responded smugly, placing her feet up on the desk.

“That was your chance. I’m coming for you. And when I’m done, you and your fucking building are going to be ashes. If you or any of your fucking minions laid a hand on Emily, I’ll peel you like an onion before you burn,” Faith informed her.

Ms. Naito dropped her feet from the desk and leaned forward in her chair.

“Come and get her,” she replied while fighting her rising anxiety.

The call ended and Ms. Naito placed the phone back in the tower with a shaky hand. She pressed the command key to lower the storage tower into the floor with her trembling finger followed by another series of command keys that brought up a hologram of Borka.

“Yes, Ms. Naito?” Borka asked like an obedient dog.

“How soon until Steel Fist is back?”

“The retrieval team is landing on the roof with him now, Ms. Naito.”

“Get him to his recharge station immediately. Faith is on her way. Meet me in the Security Chief’s office and bring the girl.”

“What do you mean on her way? And Grayson?” he asked, seemingly panicked.

“I don’t know, Borka! Did the retrieval team find any bodies?”

"The retrieval team found Steel Fist in a crater at zero percent capacity. They didn't find any buildings, let alone bodies…" Borka answered, sounding impressed.

"This doesn't leave the building, do you understand me, Borka? And send your crew in here to clean up the mess you left," Ms. Naito ordered him.

"Not a word, Ms. Naito. I'll see you…"

She cut off the call, let out a defeated screech, and pounded her fists on the desk.

Chapter 6
Now or Never

"Goddamit, Faith! What in the hell are you thinking?" Kurt asked, chastising her.

Faith lowered the phone from her ear while Grayson made a pyramid with his fingers and rested it under his nose, already working on a plan.

"It's the worst-case scenario, Kurt. Bio-Yomi has Emily. There's no other way than to tear down that building and rip her out of their arms," Faith lectured Kurt.

"You don't know that! Hell, you didn't even try to negotiate!" Kurt responded argumentatively.

"You worked under that bitch for how many years, Kurt? My dad told me all about that spoiled little shit in her ivory tower. She wouldn't have negotiated and you damn well know it," Faith responded reasonably.

Kurt rubbed his eyes with his rough fingers and let out a sigh of defeat.

"I know she's your daughter... But you have to think about this. We weren't planning on hitting that building for another six months. I'm still in talks with the other groups around the city. Besides, there's *no way* we can hit it alone. Not everyone wants to see Bio-Yomi destroyed. Two-thirds of the damned city is addicted to Vax, makes a profit off of Vax, or both. If you take down Bio-Yomi, the city is going to implode on itself. And everyone is going to be out to get the two fools that screwed them out of their livelihoods. Especially when those two fools made promises of a controlled siege with valuable loot for every gang, group, and business in the city. You burn that building down, you are burning every bridge you've made with it. Grayson, back me up, here. There *has* to be another way," Kurt pleaded with them.

Grayson sat in quiet contemplation for a moment. Kurt stared at him, desperate for a reasoned response. His eyes darted over to Faith who looked right back at him. Grayson smiled, pushed himself out of the wheelchair and onto his feet. He winced as he put weight on his injured leg and then smiled as he turned to face Kurt.

"Leave it in," Grayson stated plainly.

Kurt, confused by the statement, raised an eyebrow,

"I've decided. Leave it in," Grayson clarified as he pointed at the knife in his shin. "I'm going to get my daughter back tonight. And there's not a damn thing in this world that can stop me."

Faith smiled warmly, stood up from her chair, put her arm around Grayson, and helped him exit the kitchen. Kurt stood there, fuming.

"All right, goddammit! Wait!" Kurt hollered as he chased after them. "If you are actually going to do this, you are going to need all of the help you can get. On this short of notice, it's not going to be much."

Grayson and Faith turned to face Kurt.

"We'll take any help we can get, Kurt. And you know we appreciate it," Grayson said genuinely as he balanced his weight on Faith's shoulder.

"I know, I know," Kurt replied somewhat begrudgingly. "Now, all of the other groups and factions around Red City tolerate me because I offer them information and access to rare... *goods*. But you'd better believe that while they leave you two alone out of respect and fear, they don't like you much. I had just started negotiations trying to get key players around the city on our side for the eventual siege on Bio-Yomi. It was a rocky start but I've got one guy that *might* be willing to help. I'll give him a call on the CB radio and try to convince him that it's in his best interest."

"One's better than none, Kurt. Thank you." Faith said gratefully.

Kurt waved his hand dismissively.

"Don't thank me yet, there's no guarantee. Secondly, I've stashed a few things away in preparation for a takeover of Bio-Yomi... or to fight back a potential Government invasion. Whichever ended up coming first... Or both."

Grayson and Faith exchanged looks, unsurprised by Kurt's secret stash.

"Grayson, follow me. Faith, you have another sword, right?"

Faith paused for a moment, her heart still.

"Yes. It was made for my mother."

"Well, go fetch it and meet us down in the workshop. It's going with you tonight."

Grayson left Faith's side and used the wall as support as he followed after Kurt.

Faith returned to her studio and took a moment to take in the art she had painted on the walls as if it was the last time she would get to see it. Flowery meadows and grassy plains lined the walls as a twisting, purple night sky stretched to the ceiling, speckled with pointed stars and swirling galaxies. On the back wall behind her desk was a gorgeous cherry blossom tree with a single petal floating away with the wind.

With an inner peace and calmness, she approached the antique desk, reached behind it, and pulled out a wooden presentation box long enough to house a sword. She set the box down gently on the desk and a subtle puff of dust floated from atop the case.

With two soft "*pops*," she flipped open the latches and slowly lifted the lid of the case. On the underside of the lid, burned into the wood read:

My dearest Ann,

Though you have a dreadful battle ahead of you,

View this gift as a symbol of your strength.

You will overcome the odds if you fight with love and tenacity.

While your instinct may be to shield others from your pain,

Realize that a battle was never won with only a shield.

Your love, Bryan

Inside the case was a katana resting in a purple sheath, elegantly decorated in flowing cherry blossom petals. The handle was intricately wrapped in strips of white silk which was capped off on either end by a golden pommel and guard. As Faith slipped her fingers underneath the sheath and grip, she felt a pulsing warmth radiating from the sword. She lifted the weapon out of its case, held it in front of her, and gently unsheathed it. A blade pattern resembling crashing waves rippled down the edge of the mirror-polished steel and a glint of reflected light brushed the painted cherry blossom tree on the wall. Faith gently sheathed the sword and exited the room. She closed the door behind her, leaving the studio in complete darkness.

As Faith descended the metal staircase into the workshop, she noticed Grayson coolly leaning against the retrofitted armored truck with his arms crossed.

"Where's Kurt," Faith asked as she reached the bottom of the stairs.

"Right here, darlin'," Kurt responded as he appeared from the shadows of the back of the workshop. "I just called the potentially interested party. He'll be here momentarily to take our offer into consideration."

"Our offer?" Grayson fired back.

"You let *me* worry about that, while *you* worry about deciding what to take with you," Kurt said lightheartedly in an attempt to deflect Grayson's question.

"How about this ol' girl?" Grayson suggested while thumping the side of the armored truck with his fist.

"No, no, no," Kurt replied. "*That* is going to a very important client. We'll drive you *to*… and hopefully *from* the Bio-Yomi building in that beast. But that's it! If it gets so much as a scratch on it… Let's just say I'll have a very angry and very powerful individual ready to make my arms match my legs. For you, though, I have *this*," Kurt explained as he reached under a workbench and pressed a button.

A wall of various, roughly organized, mechanic's tools split in half and separated, revealing a hidden room. As the light flickered on, it revealed a space the size of a living area with hundreds of firearms lining the walls with a plethora of ammo cans spread across the floor.

"I knew you were a prepper, Kurt, but I didn't think you had *this* much. I can't believe you sent me out with just a six-shooter when you were hoarding this entire arsenal," Grayson exclaimed as he hobbled into the room wide-eyed like a kid in a toy store.

"Failing to prepare is preparing to fail," Kurt quipped back.

Kurt approached Faith and placed a hand on her shoulder.

"Hey now, don't think I forgot about you," he informed her with a warm smile. "Come on, now."

He beckoned her over to a nearby workbench where hand drawn schematics and a disorganized mess of tools lay strewn about. Faith followed him, lightly holding her mother's katana at her side.

"I designed this as a means for you to carve through the steel shutters of the Bio-Yomi building if they initiated lockdown while we were in there. It would be unfortunate to take over Bio-Yomi only to be locked in the building," Kurt mentioned as he trailed into a chuckle. "Granted, we will be putting this to use far earlier than expected… but it should work just fine in short bursts."

Kurt moved some schematics aside, revealing what appeared to be a heavy-duty, steel coil forged in the outline of a katana. The interior of the coil was outfitted with ventilation holes and titanium clamps. At the bottom of the device was a metal housing to place the handle of a sword into. The outside of the housing featured a rudimentary trigger and a sleek, rapier-styled handguard. In between the handguard and the coil was an empty circular ring the size of a quarter.

"Your sword, please," Kurt requested.

Faith hesitantly handed her mother's katana to Kurt as her hand struggled to release it.

Kurt removed the katana from its sheath and stared at the polished blade for a moment.

"Stunning," he said. "Just like your mother," he smiled nostalgically into Faith's reflection on the blade.

He carefully placed the grip of the katana into the fixture and clamped the blade in place. After he locked it in, he held it up and inspected the coil that now outlined the entire blade of the sword. Then, he opened a drawer in the workbench and removed a carbon-fiber cube the size of a ring box.

"Your father managed to smuggle this out of Bio-Yomi the day we left. It wasn't three days later when he showed the first signs of infection," Kurt explained despondently as he ran his thumb across the top of the cube. "I like to think he left it behind on purpose before he disappeared. Although he never mentioned it, I always felt like he left it for you."

A teardrop from Kurt's eye landed on a schematic page on the workbench. Faith placed a hand on his shoulder and squeezed.

"Let's finish this up," Kurt said, blinking his incoming tears away.

Kurt's thumb pressed a button on the cube causing the top half to separate from the bottom half. As the top floated in the air, a swirling blue ball of energy rose from the bottom of the cube. Both of their faces lit up with blue light as the radiant ball was suspended in between the two halves of the cube.

"The biomagnetic energy source. Our life's work," Kurt proudly stated.

He took a breath and slowly edged the small ball of energy toward the empty ring on the contraption that now housed the sword. The swirling ball jumped into the ring and the cube slammed shut. He set the cube down on the workbench and handed the modified katana to Faith.

Faith accepted the sword and cautiously held it away from her body, her eyes locked on the magnificent energy source swirling above the grip.

"Go on, press the trigger," Kurt suggested, fascinated to see the result of his work.

Faith's index finger hovered over the trigger, teasing it for a bit. She took a deep breath, steeled herself, and clamped down on the makeshift trigger.

The coil around the edge of the blade ferociously ignited in a wild blue flame. The fire flickered in Faith's eyes as the sapphire glow lit up the room.

Awestruck by his creation, Kurt released a jovial laugh.

"I call it Onibi! Named after a sort of… demonic ghost fire in Japanese folklore," Kurt elaborated.

Faith released the trigger and the flame extinguished.

Kurt let out a melancholy sigh as a half-smile crept across his face.

"Your father loved that crazy stuff. But, use it wisely. It has a finite amount of life to it before it needs to be recharged in the cube."

Kurt grabbed a large carbon-fiber sheath that was leaned against the workbench.

"I'll keep your mother's sheath safe for you here. Now that you have Onibi, you'll need this."

He handed her the futuristic-looking sheath and, as she moved Onibi toward it, the carbon-fiber reacted to the biomagnetic energy in the sword. The sheath came apart like a geometric puzzle and once Faith inserted the length of the katana into it, the pieces snapped onto the blade, completely encasing it.

A notification bell *dinged* from the smartphone in Kurt's apron pocket.

"With that, it appears our friend has arrived," Kurt notified Faith.

He disarmed the claymores in the alleyway outside via an app on his phone.

"You're good," Kurt shouted into the phone before pocketing it.

Faith secured the new sheath to her belt underneath her father's katana as they made their way toward the garage door, passing Grayson who was loading ammo cans into the bed of the armored truck.

"Helluva room you got there, Kurt!" Grayson hollered.

"I was saving it for a rainy day… But I guess the storm's rollin' in tonight," Kurt answered as he smacked a red button near the garage door causing the heavy door to lift.

Faith walked over to Grayson and leaned against the truck, crossing her arms and locking eyes with him.

"Cool sword," Grayson said, admiring the impressive-looking hilt poking out of the sheath.

"Jealous?" Faith asked with a smirk on her face.

Grayson reached into the bed of the truck and lifted a Barrett .50 caliber semi-automatic sniper rifle by its carry handle.

"Nope," Grayson retorted through a grin of his own.

"All right, you two," Kurt shouted from the garage door. "Come on over and meet the only guy in all of Red City willing to help you."

Faith and Grayson rounded the truck to see Kurt facing a trim, clean-cut man in a black turtle neck with a high-end Staccato 2011 pistol in a thigh holster.

"You've got to be shitting me. This fucking guy is *not* coming with us!" Grayson yelled, putting his foot down.

The man smirked, crossed his arms, and shook his head. Kurt raised his palms toward Grayson in an attempt to calm his temper.

"Now Grayson, beggars can't be choosers here. Luden is the only one who completely jumped on board with the original plan in the first place," Kurt started to explain.

"This mother fucker abandoned me in a Government resupply site in the middle of a firefight! He hopped in our extraction vehicle and took right the fuck off! I ran out of ammo and covered ten city blocks on foot to get out of there. I am *not* taking this piece of shit with me," Grayson vented.

Luden pressed his tongue into his cheek and sighed.

"Grayson, I got infected with Vola on the mission. If I wouldn't have left, I would have melted from the inside out," Luden explained defensively.

"And look at you now, a Vax addicted mess. He can't be trusted, Kurt," Grayson said before definitively walking away.

"Goddammit, Grayson," Kurt muttered as he chased after him.

Faith approached Luden confidently and looked him square in the eye.

"You still with the Psychophants?" Faith asked coldly.

"Yeah, but I'm making my move. I'm gonna scoop up all of the Vax from Bio-Yomi when we're done. I figured coming to the table with the largest stash of Vax in the city will be a one-way ticket to leadership," Luden answered honestly.

"Always in it for yourself, huh, Luden?" Faith seriously prodded.

"Is that what I'm known for nowadays?" Luden responded regretfully, staring at the floor as he rubbed the back of his head.

"I'll talk to Grayson. You're one hell of a soldier, Luden. We're lucky to have you," Faith said before turning around.

"Just tell Grayson that…" Luden began to say at the last second.

Faith half-turned to glance at Luden.

"He knows, Luden. He just doesn't care. You know how he is."

"Yeah," Luden replied under his breath.

As Faith made her way over to Grayson and Kurt who were raucously arguing with one another, Luden rolled up his sleeve and stared at the needle tracks on his arm. Memories of vomiting blood on the windshield of the getaway car the night of his infection flashed through his mind.

He blinked, making momentary eye contact with Grayson, who was now furiously debating with both Kurt and Faith on the other side of the .50 caliber turret mounted on the truck. However, the only thing he could hear were the sounds of his own panicked moans and the squealing of tires in his mind. He opened a pouch in his black cargo pants, removed a steel syringe labeled with the red Bio-Yomi arch, popped off the cap as his hand shook, and pressed the tip of the needle into the skin on the inside of his forearm. As he depressed the plunger, the sounds of his agonizing screams and the visions of his blood dripping down the interior of the windshield faded away. There was a ringing in his ears for a moment and his vision blurred. He slowly blinked and when he opened his eyes, everything was back to normal.

"I'm so sorry, Grayson," Luden whispered.

He recapped the syringe and shamefully placed it back into his pocket like a used tissue.

Grayson stormed over to the truck and opened the rear passenger-side door.

"Saddle up, Luden. But don't think I trust you for a fucking second," Grayson said threateningly before getting in and slamming the door behind him.

Faith gave Luden a thumbs-up as she climbed into the rear driver-side seat. Kurt beckoned Luden to join and tossed him the keys to the truck. The keys jingled in the air before landing in Luden's hand. As Kurt lifted himself into the passenger seat, Grayson was seething.

"I can't see how *this* could go wrong. Sure, Kurt, let the fucking deserter drive..." Grayson complained.

"Well, Grayson, it *is* his truck," Kurt said as he shrugged.

Grayson shook his head while smiling and sighing in disbelief.

Luden took a deep breath and joined them in the vehicle, easing into the driver's seat and shutting the heavily armored door behind him. Faith took Grayson's hand and placed it in her lap.

"Let's get our daughter back," Faith said as Luden started the engine with a ground-pounding rumble.

Luden popped the truck into gear and pressed his foot into the gas pedal. The motor of the truck revved into the night as they pulled out of the garage, barreled through the dark alleyway, and shot out into the darkness of Red City.

Chapter 7

One Way In

The headlights on the armored truck flipped off as Luden rolled up to the street corner facing the sixty-story Bio-Yomi building. The squeaky breaks whined to a stop as he leaned over the steering wheel to gawk at the impressive structure.

"That is hands down the cleanest building in the city," Luden waggishly mentioned in an attempt to break the silent tension in the truck.

Kurt sat forward in his seat and peered out the windshield at the neon-red arch on top of the building accompanied by the blinding white letters reading "Bio-Yomi."

"Those hoity-toity bastards have drones that fly around and clean the windows every day," Kurt informed them as he squinted up at the immaculate structure.

"Speaking of drones… They have automated turret drones patrolling the perimeter of the building as well as mounted turrets, also automated, both inside and outside of the building," Grayson irritably stated, refocusing the conversation.

Kurt reached into his apron pocket and removed four pins in the shape of the Bio-Yomi arch.

"All right everyone, take one of these. The turrets will see you as 'friendly' when you've got these on."

He passed them out and everyone immediately pinned them to their clothing.

"Oh, and Grayson? This is for you," Kurt said as he leaned into the back seat and stabbed Grayson's injured leg with a needle.

"Fuck!" Grayson yelped. "The hell did you just do?"

"It'll numb up your leg so you can actually be worth a damn out there. It'll last about an hour, but it'll hurt worse before it numbs up," Kurt clarified. "So, why don't you fill Luden and Faith in on the rest of our intel to take your mind off of it."

"Holy shit, you weren't kidding..." Grayson grunted while rubbing his leg and breathing through the pain. "So, we know that the wall around the building is damn near impenetrable. If we managed to destroy the wall, it would automatically trigger the building's lockdown procedure," Grayson continued.

"I could get us through in a pinch," Faith said as she held the grip of Onibi. "But I think we would all prefer to keep things quiet for as long as possible."

"The only entrance *and* exit to the property is the front gate. It's the only part of their perimeter that opens up and it's the only section that is short enough to scale," Kurt added as he pointed at the steel gate. "And *that*, lady and gents, is all of the intel we've gathered so far."

Luden, with both hands on the steering wheel, studied the enormous gate.

"I'll get us through the gate," Luden confidently said, staring straight ahead.

"And how in the hell are you going to do that?" Grayson asked doubtfully.

"You trust me?" Luden said, completely serious.

"*No*," Grayson instantly responded.

Luden flipped on the headlights of the truck and leisurely accelerated toward the front gate.

"When I reach the gate, you and Faith grab any weapons and ammo you need from the truck. Get in position on the side of the gate and get ready to slip through."

"What kind of shitty plan is this?" Grayson protested.

Faith placed her hand on the doorhandle and leaned into it, preparing to make her move. A bead of sweaty regret dripped down Kurt's forehead as he gulped down his anxiety.

"For fuck's sake, Luden, just drive past it and let's think about this. We can't afford to screw this up!"

"Too late, already doing it!" Luden replied as Grayson grumbled and grabbed his doorhandle.

The reflection of the headlights on the steel gate grew brighter as Luden rolled to a stop just inches away from it.

Luden drew the black, tactical 2011 from his thigh holster, removed a silencer from a large pocket in his cargo pants, and screwed it on to the threaded bull-barrel with finesse.

"All right! Move!" Luden ordered as he cracked open the driver's side door.

Faith and Grayson flew out of the vehicle and hopped up onto the rear tires on each side of the truck bed.

Faith grabbed two weighty ammo cans, hauled them to the side of the gate, and crouched down near the adjoining wall.

Grayson slung a suppressed SCAR 17 battle rifle across his chest, put his head and arm through the single-point sling of a P90 submachine gun, and heaved the semi-automatic .50 caliber sniper rifle out of the pick-up bed. He hauled ass after Faith, adjusting to his numb leg along the way, and crouched down next to her in the dark.

Luden laid on the horn of the truck while revving the engine.

"Help! I need some Vax right now! I'm fuckin' dyin' out here!" he screamed from the cracked door, convincingly sounding like a desperate tweaker.

After a moment, two blinding floodlights kicked on, illuminating the truck as the gate slowly started to slide open.

"I can't believe this is fucking working…" Grayson whispered, hesitant to be impressed.

"That has to be the slowest gate I've ever seen," Faith observed.

Two Bio-Yomi guards in tactical gear squeezed through the slot in the still-opening gate. One approached the passenger door and tapped on the thick bullet-proof window with the butt of his rifle. The other guard moved around the back of the truck and depressed the button on his radio as he rounded the driver's side.

"It's some sort of armored truck. Mounted gun on the back. Possibly our guests," the guard described over the radio.

Grayson heard a light *whirring* overhead and saw a small surveillance drone closing in on the truck.

"We have to make our move," Faith said quietly.

She lunged forward to slip through the gate, but Grayson grabbed the collar of her jacket and pulled her back.

"Look," Grayson said, concern growing in his voice.

Faith looked at the ground as the gate slid open further. She noticed a headlight beam shining through from the other side.

"Shit," she cursed while glancing over to the truck. "It's too late…"

The guard approached the cracked open driver's side door while scanning his surroundings for an ambush. He raised his rifle at the door and edged toward it.

"Outta the car, Gray…"

Luden popped out with his suppressed handgun and with a dull "*puff*," sent a 9mm hollow-point through the guard's face. His nose popped like a water balloon and wet skull fragments ejected from the back of his head. With a moist *grunt*, the guard fell to the ground as his life was snatched from him.

Hoisting himself onto the roof of the truck, Luden peeked over the top of the vehicle, and touched off another round with a suppressed "*puff*." His bullet struck the second guard in the soft tissue above his sternum from above. The round buried itself in the guard's heart, caused his knees to buckle and sent him careening into the ground.

Luden then fired into the air, striking the drone, and causing it to crash land and skid across the pavement.

"You are number *fucking* one," Luden reminded himself.

He swung back into the driver's seat from the roof, closed the door, and put it in gear. Kurt glanced at him, shocked into silence.

"Let's do this!" Luden yelled.

He stomped the gas pedal into the floor, then immediately hit the brakes, causing the truck to lurch.

"Oh, fuck…" was all he could get out.

The gate finished sliding open and Luden was staring at three Bio-Yomi assault vehicles with mounted guns pointed right at him. He slammed the truck into reverse and peeled out backwards as the mounted guns opened fire.

Kurt grabbed the dash board and shut his eyes as tightly as he could. Five large caliber rounds struck the bulletproof windshield causing it to crack as an additional volley of bullets pounded the body of the truck.

Luden spun the truck ninety-degrees, put it in drive, and accelerated down the street as the armed vehicles gave chase.

Grayson and Faith seized their opportunity to slip through the gate as it began to slide closed. They tightly rounded the corner and ran to a close-by guardhouse. Taking cover by the small building, they peeked through the window and took note of the two guards inside.

Grayson scanned his surroundings and counted fifteen guards patrolling the exterior of the Bio-Yomi building while Faith gently set down the ammo cans.

"I'm going to hop on top of this and give you some cover. Think you can quietly clear out the area?" Grayson asked.

"Have some faith," she smugly responded, fighting off a smirk.

Staying low, Faith ran off into the darkness toward the side of the building.

"Just like old times," Grayson whispered nostalgically through a smirk of his own.

Grayson left behind the .50 caliber rifle and the ammo cans as he climbed a short utility ladder on the side of the guard house. Reaching the top of the ladder, he saw a guard sitting in a folding chair facing the entrance to the Bio-Yomi building.

With light footsteps, Grayson snuck up behind the guard who began to roll up his sleeve for a fix of Vax. He retrieved the auto-knife from his pocket and with one smooth motion, deployed the blade and imbedded it deep into the guard's temple. The guard grunted and spasmed before Grayson removed the knife, retracted the blade, and left the man to lifelessly sit in the chair with blood dripping from the wound in his head.

After making a few trips up and down the ladder, Grayson had retrieved all of his gear and set up a makeshift sniper's nest. Both ammo cans laid open displaying loaded magazines for each of his various firearms. Using the dead guards backpack as a rest, Grayson went prone with the suppressed SCAR 17 battle rifle.

"Where are you at, Faith?" Grayson said to himself.

Through the riflescope, he scanned the mostly empty parking lot of the building and spied two dead guards that were face down in pools of thick blood. He found another dead guard slumped against a security vehicle. At the guard's feet were his two severed arms still gripping his rifle.

As Grayson moved his crosshairs to the wall of the building, he saw Faith quickly and quietly advancing on two more patrolling guards. He watched as Faith thrusted her father's sword at a downward angle into the guard's shoulder from behind. The guard fell to his knees, and

Faith drew her sword from his body. In the same motion, she slashed through the other guard's neck. The first guard crashed face-first into the dirt and the second guard's head fell backwards, hanging on by a string of flesh. His arterial spray pulsed onto the wall as he fell into a bush.

Faith took off into the darkness once more and Grayson continued scanning until he noticed a guard posted on the roof of another guardhouse. The guard peered through a pair of binoculars in the direction of the recently deceased bodies. As the guard reached toward the radio clipped on his shoulder, Grayson aligned the crosshairs with the guard's head, exhaled and lightly pressed the trigger. With a loud "*psht*" and a light cloud of smoke from the end of the silencer, the .308 bullet connected with the guard. Grayson watched the guard's chin shatter and explode into a fleshy mess as he fell off the roof and his body "*thumped*" onto the ground.

"Shit," Grayson muttered as he moved his scope to the entrance of the guardhouse.

The door opened and, with two well placed shots, Grayson skillfully dispatched both emerging guards; stacking their corpses in the doorway. At that moment, he heard the "*whirring*" of a small surveillance drone passing overhead.

In the Bio-Yomi building, the live feed from the drone was displayed on a large screen in the Security Chief's office.

"How did she get through? I thought you had men pursuing her vehicle?" Ms. Naito angrily asked as she nervously tapped the heel of her shoe on the tile.

"I don't have an answer for you, Ms. Naito. But she's here now," said Baker, a bald man with a blonde moustache who was wearing a nametag that read, 'Security Chief.' His rolled-up sleeves exposed a few militaristic tattoos; mementos from his career in the service.

Ms. Naito walked closer to the screen to inspect the footage more closely.

"How many guards do we have?" Ms. Naito asked in an attempt to regain control of the situation.

"We evacuated all non-essential personnel. That included all unarmed guards, so that would leave us with… sixty armed persons in the building. Sixty-six if you include your elite guard." Baker replied as he thumbed his moustache.

"Send them all after that bitch, *now*!" Ms. Naito aggressively ordered Baker.

"Pardon me, Ms. Naito, but from my count…" Baker began to say as he maneuvered the drone with a touch screen on his desk. "We've got thirty standard armed personnel left alive and currently on the premises.

On the live feed, Baker zoomed in on Faith as she chopped off a guard's arm before thrusting her sword underneath his body armor, causing the tip to poke out through the nape of his neck.

"Twenty-nine," Baker said, correcting himself. "I recommend we scramble all remaining personnel to the lobby. It's the only way in and the choke point is in our favor."

"Why do we have so few armed guards? Baker, if you fuck this up, I'll have your job. Maybe even your head…" Ms. Naito said, asserting her faux dominance over Baker.

Baker stifled a chuckle and shook his head at the ridiculousness of her threat.

"Ms., this is an R&D facility. We rely heavily on our perimeter wall and our automated turrets, which for some reason, don't seem to be targeting her."

"Fine, then do it. Send everyone downstairs!" Ms. Naito screamed as Baker reached for his radio.

Baker hesitated for a moment and apprehensively turned his chair to look at Ms. Naito.

"You know, if we reached out to the Capital location, we could lock down and await a few *hundred* reinforcements. They're actually equipped for something like this," Baker suggested.

"My father will NOT hear about this! Do you understand me?" Ms. Naito blurted out. "We can handle this. Right, *Security Chief* Baker?"

He glared at her for a second and swiveled his chair back toward the screen as the video feed suddenly cut out and turned to static.

"Looks like she's got a friend out there," Baker commented.

Ms. Naito clenched her fist as hard as she could, breaking all of the long nails on her left hand.

A *beep* sounded from the door to the Security Chief's office as Dr. Borka backed into the room with a dolly.

"What took you so long, Borka?" Ms. Naito asked furiously.

Borka spun around with the dolly that had a small stasis pod strapped to it and carefully set it down. Inside the window of the pod rested a little girl's sleeping face.

"I was tending to Steel Fist, as you asked, Ms. Naito," Borka reminded her politely.

"He'd better be ready, send him down there now!" Ms. Naito screamed, continuing to lose her cool.

"Ms. Naito, he is only at eighty-percent capacity…" Borka began to explain.

"I don't care if he's at *eight*-percent capacity! Send him *now*! We need to stamp this fire out while it can still be contained!" Ms. Naito continued to yell self-righteously.

"I am sorry, Ms. Naito. If we send him into combat at anything less than one-hundred-percent capacity, we risk corrupting his neural unit. If you think he is difficult to control *now*, imagine trying to convince the winning bidder of his capabilities when he cannot understand even the simplest of commands," Borka elucidated in an attempt to appeal to Ms. Naito's logic.

Ms. Naito looked at the girl's face through the stasis pod's window and snarled in disgust.

"Why can't anything ever be easy?" She said through a scowl. "Borka, take the girl to my office and await further orders. Baker, have the elite guard meet him there."

"Yes, Ms. Naito," Borka answered as he gently placed his hand on the stasis pod and gazed into the window for a moment.

"I'm sorry, little one," Borka whispered quiet enough so no one would hear.

Baker called for the elite guard over the radio as he brought up the main lobby cameras on the big screen. As Borka left the room with the stasis pod, Ms. Naito and Baker watched the live feed as the three elevator doors opened in the lobby and guards poured out, taking up defensive positions. Ms. Naito exhaled her stress, but it couldn't hide the worried expression on her face as she impatiently watched the screen in the painfully silent room.

Chapter 8

THRESHOLD

Faith stood at the base of a short, concrete staircase leading to the entrance of the Bio-Yomi building. The white, sterile light from the interior shined on her as she calmed her heavy breathing. With blood caked in her hair and on her clothing, she inspected the katana in her hand. Knicks, chips, and scratches decorated the blade under blotchy layers of drying blood.

She looked up from the sword and into the clear windows of the main lobby. More than twenty heavily armed guards pointed their rifles at the sliding entrance door as they stood and crouched behind pillars, counters, and furniture.

Faith turned to face the guardhouse where Grayson was set up on the roof with his rifle. Although it was nearly one hundred yards away, she could make out two guards inside violently arguing with one another and pointing at the direction of the Bio-Yomi building.

Grayson looked at Faith through his riflescope. She pointed down, held up two fingers, then pointed at him.

"Yeah, I know they're there," Grayson responded to himself as he looked over his shoulder at the claymore mine he had set up facing the ladder.

Faith motioned at the Bio-Yomi entrance and raised her hands up as if she were surrendering.

"You sure about that? There's a lot of them in there," Grayson muttered.

She sheathed her damaged and dirty sword and gave Grayson a thumbs-up.

"All right, do your thing," he mumbled through a smile.

Grayson set down his SCAR 17 and pushed aside the backpack he was using as a rifle rest. He then grabbed the .50 caliber rifle by its carry handle, deployed the bipod, and set it in front of him. Grabbing an enormous loaded magazine from a nearby ammo can, he rocked it into the magazine well, and racked a round into the chamber with a beefy "*ka-chunk.*" As he put his shoulder into the stock and adjusted the zoom of the variable scope, he took a deep breath and flicked the safety off.

"Hello, old friend," he said to the massive gun as he wrapped his fingers around the pistol grip.

He peered through the scope and had excellent visibility into the lobby through the large, clear windows. Men in black, tactical gear speckled across the spotless, white-marble lobby readied their weapons at the glass door as Faith reached the top of the concrete staircase and approached them.

As Faith reached the glass door, it automatically parted open and she crossed the threshold, entering the massive lobby. She raised her arms above her head and advanced further as the guards glanced at each other unsure of what to do. Everyone in the silent room held their breath as the sound of her boots echoed through the lobby. The hair on their arms and necks instinctively stood up at her mere presence. Twenty-seven men in full body armor pointing rifles at her from various vantage points stayed put as she progressed.

"S-stop right there!" an excitable guard hollered as he exited his cover.

The guard motioned toward a few others to join him as he cautiously approached Faith.

Faith stood still and studied her surroundings. It appeared to be a typical high-end lobby you would see in a fancy hotel featuring a towering red arch with a fountain as its base in the center of the room. A hologram that read 'Bio-Yomi' circled the arch. As she scanned, she noticed there was no emergency exit or staircase. The only way to enter the heart of the building was to take one of three elevators located at the back of the room.

With a crew of nine additional guards, the excitable guard lead the advancement toward Faith in a half-circle formation. They stopped just short of ten-feet away from her and leveled their firearms at her head.

"Female intruder is surrendering; how should we proceed?" the guard inquired into his radio.

"Just a moment on that," Baker's voice responded through the speaker of the guard's radio.

A few seconds passed as Faith shrugged her shoulders at the guard with her hands still held high and an amused smile crept across her face. The guards began to look around at each other, confused by the delay. Suddenly, the guard's radio cut back in.

"-cking shoot her *now*!" Ms. Naito's voice screamed through the mic.

The excitable guard in the center of the formation raised his rifle and put his finger in the trigger guard.

Faith's hair flew forward from a gust of wind as the guard's helmet popped off of his head like a rocket, his head liquified, and the skin from his face twisted and hung from his neck. The arch's fountain behind the guard splashed water six-feet in the air as it was struck by Grayson's over-penetrating .50 caliber bullet.

A distant, fearsome *boom* followed the bullet impact as the headless guard fell over like a stiff mannequin.

Before the remaining stunned guards could react, Faith wrapped her hand around Onibi and rushed toward the formation in front of her. Closing the ten-foot gap with swift strides, Faith pulled on Onibi's grip, causing the carbon-fiber sheath to react and separate into floating puzzle pieces. With Onibi free from the sheath, she clamped down the trigger causing the edge to ignite in a violent, scorching blue flame. The guards' fear-stricken faces lit up blue as she executed a sweeping draw-slash across their bodies. A glint of a blinding, blue light resembling a laser beam moved cleanly through all nine of their torsos. Faith released the trigger of Onibi and, with great finesse, she guided the blade back into the separated sheath. With a "*snap*," the pieces of the sheath returned to the blade and locked it into place on her hip.

All nine guards in formation began to desperately scream in agony as flames blasted from wounds in their abdomens and then from their mouths. Their eyeballs melted into thick goop that dripped down their cheeks before their burning bodies separated from their legs and fell to the ground in unison.

The seventeen surviving guards in the room looked on in terror at the pile of blazing body parts on the ground. Flames from the pile licked Faith's face as she surveyed the sheer horror on the faces of the men who witnessed her attack.

"O-open fire!" A guard's voice cracked as he took cover behind the red arch.

The muzzle of the guard's rifle flashed as he squeezed off a single shot before a gaping hole was punched clean-through the arch. His groin shredded into stringy bits and his guts fell from between his legs as he did the 'splits' and slammed to the ground. Chunks of marble exploded behind him as another one of Grayson's .50 caliber bullets slammed into the floor.

The entire room awakened into a roar of gunfire as Faith ran from cover to cover slicing and impaling her way through every guard she encountered with her father's trusty katana. The exterior glass exploded as Grayson laid down overwhelming covering fire with his hefty rifle.

Severed, leaking limbs danced through the air as blood splattered across the lobby like an abstract mural. Shouts, shrieks, and gunfire consumed the room as light fixtures came crashing down and furniture splintered. One of the security cameras was struck by an errant bullet, cutting the feed to one of the monitors in the Security Chief's office.

"No, no, no, no!" Ms. Naito screeched while kicking the back of Baker's chair as they watched the chaos unfold via the live feed. "Baker! Suit up, ready The Cannon, and get your ass down there!"

"But The Cannon is a fucking prototype… It's never even been fired in the same room as a person," Baker countered in disbelief at her request.

Ms. Naito stared pleadingly into his eyes.

"If you end this, I will double your salary."

Baker stood up from his chair, towering over the petite Ms. Naito at six and a half feet tall.

"Plus, a week off and a case of Vax," Ms. Naito added.

"Ms. Naito, for a week off… I'd kill the Pope," Baker responded, completely serious.

He coolly walked past Ms. Naito as she sat down in his chair and watched the live feed intently.

Meanwhile, Grayson's ears rang as he let loose another bullet toward the lobby. A collection of heavy spent shell casings rolled away from him as the angled muzzle-brake of the rifle expelled a powdery shockwave across the roof.

Through his scope he saw a handful of remaining guards behind a makeshift barricade in the back of the room. He leveled his crosshairs on a guard's partially exposed shoulder, squeezed the trigger, but he was met with a *click.* He reflexively removed the box magazine from the gun, reached into the ammo can for another mag, but only felt two loose rounds at the bottom. As he retrieved the two substantial .50 caliber rounds from the ammo can, he heard an argument nearby.

"I told you, I'm not fucking going up there!"

"Well, neither am I! That's *gotta* be Grayson up there!"

"That fucker's killed more people than Vola! You lost at rock, paper, scissors! You have to go!"

"Fuck that, *you* lost, *too*!"

"Yeah, but I didn't lose *fifteen times*!"

"I came outside, didn't I?"

"And now you have to go up there!"

Grayson finished loading the two remaining rounds into the large magazine, inserted it into the rifle, and racked the charging handle. He looked through the scope and saw Faith pinned down by enemy fire behind the giant red Bio-Yomi arch. One of the guards at the back of the lobby tossed a smoke grenade from behind cover, completely obscuring Grayson's view.

He stood up with the .50 caliber and peaked over the edge of the roof, spying the two arguing soldiers beneath him.

They both looked up simultaneously and made direct eye contact with Grayson.

"Oh," said one of the guards.

"Shit," said the other.

Grayson hip-fired the .50 caliber rifle, sending the first round into the chest of one of the guards. The round split his body armor in half, ripped the shirt off of his body, and blew all of his organs out his back. The second guard turned to run as Grayson fired his final round. The speeding bullet pierced shoulder-to-shoulder through the side of the guard's body, sending both of his arms flying in opposite directions, and his mashed insides pouring out of his armpit.

Smoke rose from the barrel of the rifle as Grayson dropped it onto the roof. He slung the P90 submachine gun over his shoulder as he jumped ten-feet down from the roof and landed in the dewy grass below. He recovered from the landing and sprinted past a series of dead bodies in the courtyard, hopped through the shattered entrance of the Bio-Yomi building, and jumped through the smoke to flank the guards. He hurdled dead bodies and scattered limbs in the haze, until he rounded the barricade and unleashed a full-auto torrent of armor-piercing rounds from the P90.

As the smoke cleared, Grayson saw three guards riddled with bullet holes lifelessly rag-dolled on the floor. He looked to the red arch and saw two detached arms, a rifle, and a head fly out from behind it. Faith revealed herself from behind the arch, panting heavily. With his P90 at a low-ready position, he smiled at Faith, impressed with her violent artistry.

"Gray! Behind!" Faith shouted as she ran toward him.

Grayson whipped around and looked directly down the barrel of a rifle held by the only guard left alive in the room. Before he could react, the guard yanked the trigger, but nothing happened. The guard, in a panic, flipped his rifle to the side and cursed as he verified an empty chamber.

Seizing the opportunity, Grayson held down the trigger of his P90. A single bullet fired from the short barrel, striking the guard in the gut. Grayson flinched as the P90, much to his surprise, failed to continue firing. He tilted the firearm up and confirmed that the transparent magazine was empty.

The guard discarded his rifle and drew a pistol from his thigh-holster. Grayson instinctively tossed his machine gun at the guard, hitting him in the head. He followed through, tackled the guard to the ground, and began to grapple over the handgun.

During the struggle, Grayson ejected the magazine from the gun, and frantically tried to redirect pistol away from his head.

Bang.

Grayson felt warm blood trickle down his neck from his head and watched it drip onto the guard's face. He moved his eyes further down and noticed the blade of a katana puncturing the man's throat. As blood poured from the guard's mouth and his eyes filled with fear, Grayson moved his bleeding cheek away from the edge of Faith's sword.

"Sorry, I nicked you a little, there," Faith apologized as she twisted the blade in the man's esophagus before ripping it out.

Grayson made his way back to his feet and touched the cut on his cheek while catching his breath.

"Just a scratch," he said, brushing it off.

As Faith sheathed her katana and wiped blood from her face with the sleeve of her jacket, a loudspeaker clicked on in the lobby.

"Thanks for joining the party, Grayson! Now that you've *both* arrived, I can completely remove the biggest thorn in Bio-Yomi's side… and *my* side for that matter," Ms. Naito expressed tauntingly over the loudspeaker. "So, ta-ta, farewell, and checkmate, Mommy and Daddy. I promise I'll put little Emily to good use. Naito, signing off!"

The loudspeaker cut off and the lockdown procedure for the building commenced. Indestructible metal shutters began to gradually lower over the windows and doors.

Ding.

Faith and Grayson looked over at the wide, central elevator as the doors parted revealing Baker, who was clothed head-to-toe in a bomb-disposal suit retrofitted with bulletproof armor panels. In front of him was an oversized mounted gun, resembling a futuristic cannon, that was bolted to the floor of the elevator. Faith recognized a small biomagnetic energy source that was swirling in an attached ring-slot on the side of the carbon-fiber cannon.

Baker's blonde moustache tilted to one side through the window of his helmet as he cracked a blood lusting smile from behind The Cannon. He flipped open two protective caps on the device's handle, and mashed his thumbs down on the mechanical buttons underneath.

Grayson shielded Faith and drew his .44 magnum revolver from his jacket, pointing it directly down the barrel of the cannon as it began to glow with a blue, fiery energy. Grayson noticed a light in the corner of his eye as the sound of a powerful engine grew louder.

Turning their heads to look, Grayson and Faith saw Kurt behind the wheel of Luden's armored truck as it smashed through a large window. Sparks flew from the roof of the truck as it barely cleared the metal shutter on its way down. The truck's suspension flexed as it landed inside the lobby and the tires squealed as Kurt slid the armored vehicle in between Grayson and The Cannon at the last second.

Kurt dove into the backseat as a devastating blue, fiery beam exploded from the elevator and slammed into the driver's side door, melting it away and popping the front tire of the truck.

Baker's smile stretched ear-to-ear from the raw power of his weapon as his face glowed blue.

Luden popped up from the bed of the truck, hopped onto the mounted .50 caliber turret, and swung it around to face Baker.

Baker desperately tried to swivel The Cannon, but Luden had him beat. All Baker could do was flinch and instinctively shield his face with one of his hands.

Rhythmic, concussive "*thumping*" pounded the room as Luden unleashed a barrage of high-caliber rounds from the mounted Browning M2 machine gun. Weighty, spent shell casings pelted the roof of the truck as Baker's suit was shredded by the bullets, sending chunks of his body bouncing around the elevator like wet popcorn. Two rounds hit The Cannon, igniting it in a blue blaze before exploding and sending the elevator into a freefall down the shaft.

There was a blinding flash in the elevator shaft followed by silence as Luden ceased firing.

"Woo!" Luden howled victoriously.

Grayson released Faith from his protective grasp as Luden hopped down from the bed of the truck.

"What do you think, Grayson? Are we square now?" Luden proudly asked, holding his arms out at his sides.

He then fell backwards into the side of the truck and landed on his butt.

Grayson rushed over to Luden, noticing his leg was tied off with a tourniquet and he had a gunshot wound in his lower abdomen.

"Goddammit, Luden, what happened?" Grayson asked as he knelt down to get a closer look at his wounds.

"Grayson, go get your damn daughter back so this wasn't all for nothing. But I swear to God, we'd better be fucking even now," Luden lectured Grayson through waves of pain as he held pressure on his abdominal wound.

Grayson stood up and turned away from Luden. He glanced back and firmly gave him a nod. Luden contentedly returned the nod with an injured smile.

Faith rounded the destroyed vehicle and helped Kurt crawl out of the truck. One of his prosthetic legs had been blown off by the blast from The Cannon, so he balanced himself on a single leg.

Kurt surveyed the destroyed room filled with mutilated bodies and buckets of blood.

"You guys did some damage!" Kurt exclaimed.

Faith let go of Kurt as he held himself up on the bed of the truck.

"And *you guys* need to get the hell out of here," Faith replied as she approached one of the lockdown shutters.

She drew Onibi from its sheath, ignited the sword, and unleashed an overhead slash at the metal shutter causing it to melt away like a burning spiderweb.

Faith sheathed Onibi and returned to Grayson's side as Luden stood up from the ground and put Kurt's arm over his shoulders.

"I know a guy down the street who can patch us up. You two just bring Emily home safe, you hear?" Kurt said as Luden helped him toward the sliced-open shutter.

Faith confidently nodded to Kurt as Grayson placed his hand on her back and guided her toward the elevators.

"See you around, Grayson!" Luden hollered as he walked away and flashed a goodbye-wave over his shoulder.

Grayson and Faith pressed the 'up' button for one of the functioning elevators and with a "*ding*" the elevator doors opened. They took a breath and stepped inside. As they turned around to inspect the panel of buttons, the doors closed and the elevator jolted up.

"It seems like someone knows exactly where we're supposed to be," Grayson jokingly deduced as he watched the floor numbers rapidly climb on the overhead display.

"Wherever these doors open, the odds will be against us. As per the usual," Faith predicted as she crossed her arms and leaned her back against the wall of the elevator.

Grayson did a few little hops while shaking his arms and head in an attempt to shrug off the previous battle and hype himself up.

"Come on, you missed this a little bit," Grayson suggested as he cracked his neck. "Causing trouble for Bio-Yomi, fighting for a righteous cause..."

"Another time, another life, Grayson. Now I'm just a mom mowing down anything in the path of my baby," Faith responded as she tapped the toe of her boot into the elevator floor.

"Yeah, I missed it a little bit, too," Grayson nonchalantly replied.

Faith turned her head, trying to hide a smile.

The overhead display stopped on floor sixty and emitted a "*ding*."

"Let's bring our daughter home," Grayson affirmed as he squeezed the grip of his revolver tightly.

Chapter 9

Reunions

As the elevator doors opened, Grayson and Faith were met by six guards in heavy, white, tactical gear pointing rifles at them from twenty feet away. Grayson raised his revolver and placed his finger on the trigger.

"Now, now, Grayson… That's a sure way to get your daughter killed," Ms. Naito proudly announced as she theatrically pushed aside two of her elite guards to stand between them. "Don't be shy, come on out of the elevator. It can't go anywhere without my permission anyway. You are stuck," she continued.

Grayson lowered his gun as he and Faith hesitantly stepped into the small reception area and surveyed their surroundings.

Several fancy waiting chairs lined the wall across from a glass reception desk. To their left was a dead end featuring an extravagant bust of Hirohiko Naito, the founder of Bio-Yomi and father of Kimberly Naito. To their right was a long, sterile hallway lined with doors requiring security clearance. Directly in front of them was another hallway that lead directly to Ms. Naito's office, which was currently being blocked by Ms. Naito and her elite guards.

"I have been imagining meeting you face-to-face for so long, Grayson. The man who nearly dismantled Bio-Yomi in a single night," Ms. Naito pontificated as she paced in front of her guards. "The *Gray Ghost*! That's what they call you around here. Did you know that? Not only did you massacre our employees at every single vaccine site on Vax Day, but you managed to plant a bomb on a helicopter that detonated as it landed on Bio-Yomi's Capital City headquarters. It would have killed my father if he wouldn't have been at a press conference across town. Have you seen Bio-Yomi's bounty on you? Have you seen the *Government's*?"

Grayson and Faith stared at her in silence, waiting for an opportunity to strike.

Ms. Naito, noticing the silence, stretched out her arms and seductively moved her fingers in a 'bring it on' motion.

"All right, time for questions. I know you've got so many of them just *eating* you up inside."

Grayson nervously ran his thumb across the serrations on the hammer of his revolver.

"Where's Emily?" Grayson probed through gritted teeth.

"In my office... Why? Are you going to do something stupid Grayson?" Ms. Naito confidently inquired. She crossed her arms and looked him up and down. "I think he's going to do something stupid. Rope him."

One of the elite guards fired a steel rope from an under-barrel attachment on his rifle. The metal lasso wrapped around Grayson's torso and arms several times before cinching down tightly, causing Grayson to release his revolver. The guard yanked the rope back, causing Grayson to crash into the ground.

Faith quickly reached for Onibi's grip, but froze as Ms. Naito held up a hand.

"I wouldn't do that if I were you. *He* was the only one with a lasso. If you did anything rash… they'd just have to kill you," Ms. Naito explained condescendingly as the remainder of her personal guard trained their weapons on her. "Next question, Grayson," she ordered him, clearly relishing the moment.

Grayson struggled on the floor, attempting to escape from the rope to no avail. With veins bulging from his neck he looked up at Ms. Naito.

"Give me back my daughter! We'll fucking kill you all!" Grayson shouted as the steel rope began to slice into his skin.

"Grayson, if you don't ask me another *question*, I'll have you shot where you lay," Naito responded with a sharpened tone.

He took a moment to consider his options as his eyes frantically searched for a way out.

"Why did you take her? Was it because of me?" he asked angrily with spittle flying from his mouth.

"Well, yes, actually. But not for the reason you think. You gave little Emily the vaccine when she was a baby, did you not?" Ms. Naito prodded through an ear-to-ear grin.

"Grayson?" Faith asked as confusion washed over her face.

"Oh, she doesn't know," Ms. Naito observed with great interest. "Do you want to tell her or should I?"

Tears fell from the corners of Faith's eyes.

"You said it wasn't Vola, Grayson! You said she was fine!"

"Goddammit, Faith… I'm sorry, but you couldn't know! No one could know! They would have taken her from us! Carlton brought me the Vax… and I…" Grayson trailed off.

Ms. Naito giggled, truly reveling at her position of power.

"Oh, lovely little Carlton. He told me *all* about it! How he brought the syringe… How you injected it into your poor, sick baby… How she had *no negative reaction to the vaccine*," she coyly mentioned.

"*What*?" Faith whispered in disbelief. "Grayson, what is she talking about?"

"I'm sorry, Faith. She was going to die. I had no choice. I gave her the Vax and then she was fine. She didn't crave more... It's like she was never sick," Grayson shamefully explained.

Ms. Naito clapped her hands together and snickered through closed lips.

"I'm sure you can imagine there are many benefits to slicing her open and reverse engineering whatever happened inside of that interesting little body of hers," Ms. Naito stated villainously just to toy with them.

Thud.

Thud.

Thud.

Recognizing the ominous sound, Grayson and Faith looked to their right to see the behemoth, Steel Fist, menacingly approaching from the side hallway accompanied by Dr. Borka.

"We stalled long enough. Kill the bitch and bring Grayson to my office," Ms. Naito indifferently ordered as she turned and walked away.

The lasso guard started to drag Grayson away as he fought to keep Faith in his line of sight.

Two guards fired three controlled rounds at Faith as she reflexively drew her father's katana, slashing the first bullet out of the air. A second round struck her below the left breast, blowing pieces of her leather jacket out her back. The third round entered just below her right collar bone, causing her to recoil in pain. Both guards lowered their rifles as Steel Fist closed in on her.

"Faith! God, *NO*!" Grayson helplessly screamed as he was dragged down the hallway.

Faith turned to face Steel Fist, who was cocking his bulky, mechanical arm back as he advanced. His carbon-fiber patterned poncho rippled behind him with each step he took.

Thud.

Thud.

Thud.

"Grayson, *took*!" screamed the hulking monster through his unruly metal teeth.

Staggered by the gunshots, but with a surge of pure adrenaline, Faith raised her katana and thrust it toward Steel Fist's arm.

Steel Fist released his punch and his knuckles connected with the tip of Faith's katana, resulting in a tiny spark. The sword deeply flexed before snapping in two. Faith instinctively closed her eyes and turned her head away as the sword shattered, causing the tip to launch back and impale her left bicep.

As she grimaced from the pain, Steel Fist wrapped his three remaining human fingers on his left hand around her throat and lifted her off the ground. He turned her around to face the right-side hallway and inspected her closely in the light.

Faith mustered all of the energy she could to look toward Ms. Naito's office. Through her fuzzy vision she saw Grayson on the ground shouting at her, though she couldn't hear it. The doors to the office closed behind Grayson's soundless screams and he disappeared from her sight. Beginning to lose consciousness, she looked at Steel Fist's face. His robotic eye was steady and unwavering, while his baby-blue human eye sorrowfully studied her face.

In a final act of survival, Faith thrust what remained of her broken sword into Steel Fist's human arm. Although blood dripped down the jagged blade, he did not react.

"Grayson *took*," the creature mumbled once more in a raspy tone.

Steel Fist cocked his battering-ram of an arm once more.

"*I* take…" he concluded mournfully.

Faith closed her eyes and imagined holding Emily tightly in her arms.

Releasing his roaring fist, he punched Faith directly in her chest, and sent her flying out of his grip down the side hallway. Her body limply impacted the ground and slid across the floor before coming to a lifeless stop.

Steel Fist transferred his attention from Faith's body to Borka, who was still standing near the entry of the hallway.

"Good work, Steel Fist! Now go to Ms. Naito's office. That's where *Grayson* is," Borka explained to the creature, as if talking to a stupid dog.

The half-mechanical monstrosity turned and made his way, with heavy footsteps, toward Ms. Naito's office.

Borka ran toward Faith's crumpled body, his footsteps echoing through the empty hallway. He knelt down, gently touched her cheek, and turned her head to face him. One of her eyelids flickered as she wheezed for air through her blood-filled mouth.

"Looks like you've got some fight left in you," Borka observed as he grabbed the collar of her jacket and began to drag her body down the hallway. "Stay with me for a few moments more, the lab is just ahead."

As Borka arrived at a dead end, he released Faith's collar, and pressed a white tile in the wall. A small slot opened in the tile and a needle extended, pricking Borka's hand. Borka removed his hand from the wall and rubbed the mark on his palm.

"DNA match confirmed," an automated voice chimed. "Welcome, Dr. Borka."

Borka dragged Faith into the hidden doorway as it seamlessly closed behind them.

On the other side of the building, Grayson sat defeated on his knees in the center of Ms. Naito's vast, white office. Her six elite guards lined the side-walls in the office, professionally awaiting her next order.

After noticing that Emily was nowhere to be seen, he lazily scanned the room and noticed chips in the tile along with faint bloodstains deep in the marble floor. As his gaze shifted up, he peered out the spotless window overlooking the entirety of Red City. The perspective engulfed his thoughts as he realized that the famously blood-stained streets were largely painted red by his own hands.

"You're quiet, Grayson," Ms. Naito mentioned as she eased back in the elegant chair behind her desk. "Have I *broken* the most fearsome terrorist in the country?"

Grayson sluggishly looked up and stared at Ms. Naito with conquered eyes.

"The way I see it, you've taken away everything I loved. There's no need to make a thing out of it... I'm dead where I sit," Grayson explained crestfallenly.

"You're not dead, Grayson, but you will be soon," Ms. Naito responded frankly.

The doors to her office parted as the seven-foot tall Steel Fist ducked his head, turned sideways, and entered the room. With cumbersome footsteps, he forebodingly walked around Grayson and turned to face him. Although the oversized fiend had no lips, Grayson could tell he was smiling at him.

"Did you handle her, as ordered?" Ms. Naito questioned.

"I... *took...*" Steel Fist groaned with satisfaction.

Grayson's heart sank deep into the pit of his stomach and his face turned pale and numb.

"You don't recognize him, do you?" Ms. Naito observed arrogantly. "I mean, how could you? Look at what you've *done* to him."

Grayson examined Steel Fist closely, hunting for a single recognizable feature.

"Do you know why I made him like this?" Ms. Naito asked rhetorically. "It was my idea to weaponize prosthetics. Well, perhaps it wasn't *my idea*, but I was the only one with the balls to get it done. My father is... ambitious... in his own right, but he always said that creating weapons would draw too much attention to his other dealings. Steel Fist, remove your covering, would you?"

Steel Fist grabbed his poncho with the three human fingers on his left hand, ripped it from his body, and tossed it to the side. His torso was an amalgamation of metal, skin, tubes and wires stemming from a huge biomagnetic energy source swirling in the center of his chest. Grayson felt a short pulse of pain from the dagger that was still imbedded in his shin, which he now realized had been launched through Steel Fist's energy source.

Along Steel Fist's back were vertical rows of syringes traveling down either side of his spine with the needles stuck in his skin. Grayson watched as a plunger on one of the syringes near Steel Fist's shoulder depressed, causing Steel Fist to momentarily shut his human eye and choppily exhale.

From the waist down, Steel Fist was purely synthetic. He had two robotic legs the size of short telephone poles complimented by feet resembling anvils.

"He's an intriguing specimen, is he not? His arm, face, and chest were the only things that needed to be replaced at first," Ms. Naito rambled. "But his legs couldn't support the weight of his other augments, so we exchanged those as well."

Grayson was still racking his brain, trying to come up with the hulking creature's identity.

"You see, Grayson, because of your attacks on Bio-Yomi property and the assassination attempt on my father, you have the single highest bounty on your head out of anyone in the Bio-Yomi Territories," Ms. Naito began to explain while leaning back and resting her heels on her clear desk. "Because of that, I am going to record a fight between you, the *fearsome* Gray Ghost, and my weaponized creation, Steel Fist. With this recording, I will destroy my father's would-be assassin, relieve him of a pricey bounty, and prove to him the usefulness of my work here."

Steel Fist clenched his three fingers and squinted his eye at Grayson.

"Steel Fist here is a prototype… A proof of concept, if you will. He was a necessary stepping stone, but soon he'll be more useful to me as a pile of cash," Ms. Naito explained as she swiped a finger across her desk, lowering four shielded cameras in each corner of the room.

"I've already kicked off the auction to acquire this *impressive*, weaponized man. Russia, China, North Korea… After I send this recording to the interested parties… perhaps even the U.S. Government will toss a shadow-bidder into the mix. I've heard their bounty for you is nearly as high as Father's. If Steel Fist can kill you, he can kill *anyone*. *That'll* put their trepidations to rest."

Grayson just shook his head and sat back on his ankles.

"And what will you do when they use him against you?"

Ms. Naito belted out a psychotic laugh.

"By the time I'm done with your daughter, Steel Fist may as well be a soda can to me. Now, stop stalling and *fight* already!"

"You may as well order your guards to just shoot me, because I'm not going to fight him," Grayson said resolutely. "I'm not going to be your fucking gladiator."

Ms. Naito rose from her chair and pressed a key on her desk. A hidden door opened in the wall behind her, revealing a dark storage space. She rose from her seat and approached the hidden area.

"As Father says, the weak are always *so* predictable," Ms. Naito declared as she reached into the hidden room.

She grabbed the handles of a dolly, wheeled it out and set it down next to her desk.

Grayson's eyes grew wide as he saw, on the dolly, the face of his daughter in the window of a stasis pod.

"Emily! EMILY!" Grayson yelled at the top of his lungs.

In a fit of rage, Grayson fought to break the steel rope around his body, managing to somewhat loosen it. He struggled to his feet and took a half-step forward.

Ms. Naito pressed a key on her desk, lowering the machine gun turret from the ceiling. Grayson froze in horror as the turret locked onto the stasis pod. He stared at Emily's peaceful, sleeping face as he ceased fighting to remove the restraint.

"I want a good fight Grayson, so I offer you this: If you defeat Steel Fist, I will give you a *chance* to save your daughter. We will inject you with Vax to see if the mutation is genetic. If it is, we will have no need for your child and you can take her place."

Grayson stared at Ms. Naito with a raging fury.

"You can shove that deal up your ass. I'm going to kill this fucking thing, and then I'm going to kill you and all of your little minions here. Then, I'm going to send the recording to your father so he can watch you die like a piece of shit hiding behind a child."

Ms. Naito couldn't hide her satisfied smile. She then motioned at one of the elite guards.

"Let him loose, it's showtime!" Ms. Naito called out to the guard while clapping her hands twice above her head. "And do *not* interfere with the fight. I want Father to see what I can do."

The guard who had captured Grayson pressed a button on the side of his rifle's under-barrel attachment, causing the steel wire to snap and break free.

Grayson glanced once more at Emily as he shook the blood flow back into his arms. He closed his eyes for a moment envisioning a warm reunion with his daughter. Reopening his eyes, he squared up to Steel Fist and pierced his human eye with a glare of death. They began to circle one another in the center of the room like two lions preparing to fight.

"*Grayson... Took,*" Steel Fist angrily muttered as they sized each other up.

Ms. Naito raised the clear shield in front of her desk with the press of a button.

"Still haven't figured it out, Grayson?" Ms. Naito yelled from behind her shield. "You killed eighty-eighty people on Vax Day and only one of them wasn't a Bio-Yomi employee."

Suddenly, the memory came rushing back to Grayson. He saw Carlton sitting at the kitchen table.

"I NEED MORE, GRAYSON!" Carlton desperately screeched.

He remembered Faith holding Carlton down on the floor of the kitchen while he kicked open a military supply crate in the living area of the run-down apartment.

"Grayson, don't go!" Faith pleaded as she restrained a squirming Carlton.

He lifted a .50 caliber sniper rifle from the crate and proceeded to toss loaded magazines and loose cartridges into a backpack.

"I'm not letting more of that fucking poison hit the streets," Grayson said, putting his foot down.

As it all came back to him, Grayson recalled setting up on the tenth floor of an apartment building with a vantage point over a mobile vaccination site. Three lines that were nearly one-hundred people long, lined up outside a white RV with a red Bio-Yomi decal on the side. With a "*thump*" on the windowsill, he rested the long barrel of the rifle on the edge of the broken window.

"I hear three Vax sites were completely demolished within the last hour," claimed a man in a white bio-hazard suit outside the RV.

"It comes right from the fucking top; we get this vaccine out to as many people as we can tonight. No exceptions," another man in a bio-hazard suit replied.

Placing his crosshairs on the first man in the containment suit, Grayson squeezed the trigger. With an earsplitting "*boom*," the man was cut in half by the bullet, turning the other man's white suit completely red.

Boom! Grayson fired again, folding the second man's body into a limp pile of meat.

Everyone in line waiting for the vaccine panicked and began to scramble, scream and trample their way out of the area except for one man.

A bulky male in a blue shirt crashed through the panicked crowd and rushed into the RV. He exited with an entire case of the vaccine on his shoulder and sprinted down the street. Grayson tracked the man's head with his scope.

"Goddammit, put it down. Don't make me…" Grayson said to himself.

He noticed he was about to lose sight of the man as he neared a street corner. Making a quick decision, Grayson hurriedly moved the crosshairs from the man's head to the crate and squeeze the trigger.

The bullet instead struck the man's arm, blowing it clean off, and sending the crate and his body crashing to the ground. Grayson slammed his eyes shut, reopened them, and found himself facing off against Steel Fist in Ms. Naito's office.

"He was the only one who survived the Gray Ghost that night. His entire family was infected with Vola, it's truly a shame," Ms. Naito informed him. "He had a cure, Grayson, right there in his hands and you took that from him. While we… *repurposed* him, his wife, his children, his parents, all died horrific, unspeakable deaths. And it's all your fault."

"Maybe it is. But I lost my brother and my wife tonight. I'm not going to lose my daughter, too," Grayson declared.

He looked once more into Steel Fist's blue eye that was filled with a sorrowful rage.

"Grayson… took… FAMILY," the creature bellowed as the swirling blue energy in his chest spun faster.

Steel Fist planted his dense feet in the ground, causing the flooring to crack beneath him as he cocked his arm back and released a shattering roar that reverberated through the room. The guards nervously looked at each other.

"Bring it *on*, mother fucker!" Grayson taunted.

CHAPTER 10

HIJACKED

"Faith! Faith, my dear! Open your eyes," Dr. Borka called out while snapping his fingers in front of Faith's nose.

Her eyes slowly opened and she saw Borka's face inches from hers. She glanced down and realized she was strapped to a metal table and had all kinds of tubes and wires sticking out of her. Shocked, she flinched and jerked her body causing the table to wobble.

"Faith! Be calm, now! I will help you save your Emily, yes?" Borka said soothingly.

Faith's heart continued to race even though she stopped moving.

"Where…" Faith started to ask before her own coughing and wheezing interrupted her.

"There is not much time for you, so you must make a decision while I power it up," Borka said as he darted around the room checking on multiple monitors.

Faith nodded her head and produced a wet cough of understanding.

As she looked down at the tubes and machines hooked up to her, a memory of visiting her mother in the hospital as a toddler rushed into her mind. She remembered walking up and grabbing her mother's cold hand and studying her lifeless face. Her father wiped tears from his cheeks as he spoke to the doctor.

Dr. Borka walked near her once more and began to pace back and forth.

"Years ago, your father developed the biomagnetic energy source with his partner. You know this, I'm sure, based on that sword of yours," Borka glanced at a nearby medical tray on which Onibi was balanced in its sheath. "I knew your father well. Though he did not think much of me, I liked him."

Faith winced in pain as she gasped for breath.

"Yes, yes, to the point. Mr. Naito wanted us to find a way to use the biomagnetic energy source to power the human body. It would act as a... prosthetic heart. We knew it produced enough energy to power and regenerate all of the organs in the human body, including hair, skin, and nails, for roughly a month's time before needing a charge. No need to sleep, no need to eat, it would act as a rechargeable battery, if you will. And, as long as you have access to a Bio-Yomi charging station, it would last *indefinitely*. Not only would you gain several hours a day by skipping meals and sleep... It would be true immortality. But here is the catch: while it has the capacity to *power* and *regenerate* the body... It cannot do so for more than five minutes without a compatible conductor."

A monitor beeped and steam was released from a large capsule behind Faith. She attempted to get a better look at it, but recoiled as excruciating pain stabbed her in the chest. Borka looked at the large capsule, tapped a few keys on the monitor's touch screen, and began to increase the cadence of his speech.

"You see, we developed a DNA-plasmid vaccine with the intention of altering a person's DNA to naturally produce cells that would act as conductors for the biomagnetic energy source. However, the closest we got to success was a vaccine that *teased* the DNA, but did not change it. Once the DNA was teased in that direction, over time it would reverse, withering away and becoming damaged. The only way to repair it was to continuously introduce the vaccine, thus resulting in behavior that mimicked addiction. Although there were several of us on the team capable of developing DNA altering technology, none of us were experts in the field."

"Ninety-nine percent capacity, prepare subject for pairing," an artificial voice chimed from the capsule.

Borka began to remove the wires and tubes from Faith as he continued to speak.

"We were stumped and Mr. Naito saw an opportunity in the worldwide desperation concerning the Vola virus. He poached all of the researchers around the world who had nearly reached a vaccine for the Vola virus and gave them… morally questionable resources to perfect it. At the same time, he consulted the recently hired experts about our biomagnetic conductor vaccine. The general consensus was that there were too many variables, and that we would have to rely on luck, genes, and mutation to unlock the puzzle. This is when Mr. Naito forced the researchers to combine our biomagnetic conductor vaccine with their completed Vola vaccine to get it into as many human bodies as possible in hopes of finding successful DNA alteration among the millions of subjects. It appears your daughter is the first and only person to see complete DNA mutation. Her DNA was not merely *teased*... It was permanently altered. It *adapted*. If we injected her with the biomagnetic conductor vaccine... Well, let's just say she is, quite literally, the key to immortality. Ms. Naito got her hands on Emily first, and now she is trying to secure the power of immortality for herself. She has kept the little one a secret from Mr. Naito for this very reason. She is in a difficult position, however, because we need her father's researchers to reverse-engineer Emily's mutation... which would be *lethal* to little Emily. Even if I *could* do it on my own, I simply would not."

The pressurized doors to the capsule separated as Borka undid the straps holding Faith to the table. He put her arm over his shoulders and lifted her up.

"Project Izanami, ready for pairing," the artificial voice echoed from the capsule.

As Faith looked into the capsule, she saw a mechanized suit of polished black armor. There was no torso section of the suit, but it consisted of arms, legs, and a helmet with a golden visor. The arms of the suit feature spiked elbows and razor-sharp claws curling from the knuckles. A mechanical spinal column connected the helmet to the limbs and, attached to the back of the shoulder blades, were two large vents reminiscent of triangular turbine engines. In between the vents spun a churning, blue energy source.

"Remember when I said you had a choice to make?" Borka asked rhetorically. "Ms. Naito had me create this suit for her to make her an invulnerable… how did she put it… *goddess of death.* Once she achieved immortality, stepping into this suit would instantly make her the most powerful force on the entire planet. But, for you, there is a catch… If you get into this suit without an internal biomagnetic energy source, the suit's external source will only power it for five minutes. That is why we have programmed automatic Vax injections into Project Steel Fist's operation. The whole reason Steel Fist was created in the first place was to *prove* that a human could be weaponized with an energy source before Ms. Naito proceeded with her plans… *against* her father's orders, I might add. While Steel Fist was a success, his destructive powers were too great and his behavior was too unpredictable. As long we can keep the DNA tease going, we can keep him functional for about an hour… but we only have so much control over his actions."

"Do… it…" Faith weakly whispered.

"You may want me to finish first… Once you are paired to Project Izanami, the suit will become permanently attached to you. Its external energy source will power, regenerate, and heal your body while it is active, but once it powers down, you will lose the effect and it will have to be surgically removed… Not a big deal for someone with natural regenerative abilities as Ms. Naito intended… But deadly to an average human. So, now that you know the risks…

Faith grabbed Borka by his lab coat with her bloody hand and nodded, accepting her fate.

Borka lifted her into the capsule and leaned her against the spinal column of the suit.

"Why?" Faith squeaked out in pain.

He smiled and said, "I experiment on criminals and the scum of Red City… not little girls. Besides, no one should have that kind of power. Especially not Bio-Yomi."

His expression became stoic as he leaned closer to Faith.

"Ms. Naito is a self-interested individual and if left to her devices… immortality would begin and end with her. *Mr.* Naito, however, is calculated… intelligent… strategic… He must *not* obtain this power. At *any* cost. I do not trust Ms. Naito to keep it from falling into his hands."

Borka walked over to a three-monitor setup and initiated several commands.

The capsule to the door closed as it filled with steam.

"Project Izanami, pairing initiated," the artificial voice announced.

"I am sorry Faith, this will not be pleasant," Borka said under his breath.

With the press of a command key, thick needles shot out from the spinal column of the suit, imbedding themselves deep into Faith's back. She screamed in agony as the suit forcefully clamped around her arms and legs.

From the back of the helmet, a long needle pierced the base of Faith's skull, silencing her screams. A display appeared on the visor in front of her eyes showing a progress bar of the pairing process. It showed twenty-two percent and climbing. As she moved her eyes around, she noticed she was seeing everything in thermal vision. The biomagnetic energy source on the back of the suit began to whirl and spin faster, causing the needles to glow blue. Faith's muscles contracted as her wounds began to close and strength returned to her body.

Borka grabbed the sheathed Onibi from the table and clutched it with both hands as he waited.

Chapter 11

FACEOFF

Grayson juked to the left, deftly dodging another rocketing punch from Steel Fist's boulder of a hand. He flanked behind the metallic abomination and studied his body for weaknesses as it recovered from the whiffed strike.

"Is that all you've got you big bastard?" Grayson yelled, taunting Steel Fist.

He took note of every fleshy patch of skin Steel Fist had left and eyed the Vax syringes lining his back.

"Goddammit you stupid machine! Stop toying with him! Show everyone what you're made of!" Ms. Naito irritatingly commented from behind her clear shield.

The elite guards lining the room tracked Grayson with their rifles in case he pulled a fast one and attacked them or Ms. Naito.

Steel Fist growled and turned to square off against Grayson once more. As Steel Fist rested his brutish arm at his side, the large hydraulic piston compressed and locked into place. With impressive speed, Steel Fist raised his arm to attack. "*Whoosh, whoosh, whoosh!*" Three fatal punches rapidly launched toward Grayson as the mechanical arm was repeatedly propelled forward by the hydraulic system. Grayson narrowly dodged the strikes like a seasoned boxer, casually stepped back, and shrugged.

"They ought to change your name to Bitch Fist after that," Grayson quipped, goading Steel Fist into a more substantial attack.

The hulking creature howled, compressed the hydraulic piston on his knuckles in addition to the one on his arm.

"*GRAYSON!*" Steel Fist thundered as he cocked his arm.

Grayson rushed toward Steel Fist as the mechanical man took a stride forward and released a mighty haymaker toward his head. Grayson then dove feet-first underneath the punch, slid in between Steel Fist's legs, and popped up behind him.

He quickly reached into his pocket, deployed his switchblade, and jammed the knife into the back of Steel Fist's metallic knee. Twisting and turning the knife in a bundle of wires and cables, blue steam shot from the joint like a leaking propane tank. Steel Fist dropped to one knee and caught himself from falling forward with his human hand.

Grayson used Steel Fist's heel as a step and boosted himself onto his back. He scaled Steel Fist's spine, dislodging and knocking loose Vax syringes that clanked onto the ground. Reaching the massive shoulders, Grayson reached around with his knife and jammed the pointed blade into Steel Fist's human eye. The knife effortlessly sliced into the eyeball, splitting it in half before Grayson twisted and pulled it out.

The guards peeked over their rifles in disbelief as Ms. Naito slammed her palms onto her desk, shot out of her chair, and stood frozen in shock.

Steel Fist produced a deep, guttural screech as he stood up and clutched his sliced-open eye that was now oozing blood. Grayson followed up by jabbing the blade into Steel Fist's clavicle and attempted to pull it back out to no avail.

In a blind rage, Steel Fist reached back and grabbed Grayson by the arm, and slammed him into the ground with an overhead smash. With the wind knocked out of him, Grayson quickly rolled to the side as the giant arm smashed into the ground next to him. He stared, for a moment, at the crater in the floor next to him before attempting to scramble away.

Steel Fist grabbed the dagger still imbedded in Grayson's shinbone and dragged him closer, eventually lifting him off the ground by the handle of it.

The behemoth roared as he cocked his arm and launched a punch at the dangling Grayson. Reflexively, Grayson blocked his head with his arm in an attempt to shield himself from the punch.

The steel knuckles connected with Grayson's elbow, shattering all of the bones in his arm. He flew across the room and smashed into the wall between two guards who dodged out of the way at the last moment. As Grayson impacted the ground, he gasped for air as the pain of his crushed, limp arm overwhelmed him. He slowly made his way to his feet and looked up at Steel Fist who still had the dagger in his hand.

Ms. Naito sat back down in her chair and took a breath.

Grayson, letting his broken arm loosely dangle, inspected his leg and watched blood pool on the floor from his leaking shin.

Steel Fist rushed him once more, unleashing a flurry of slices with the dagger in his left hand and punches with his powerful right arm. Grayson tried his hardest to avoid the strikes while backstepping and circling the towering beast. He managed to escape several punches, but he could not avoid getting sliced and poked by the dagger.

As Grayson finally began to run out of steam, a punch connected sending him into the floor with great force. On his back and out of gas, he looked up at Steel Fist who looked down at him with his remaining robotic eye as a steady stream of blood poured from his wounded eye.

Grayson unsteadily reached into his jacket pocket and pulled out Emily's beaded bracelet. He wrapped it tightly around his fingers.

"I'm… sorry," he murmured while taking one final look at Emily's peaceful face through the window of her pod.

Steel Fist compressed the large hydraulic piston in his arm, followed by the piston attached to his knuckles. Then, Grayson looked at Steel Fist's bicep and watched as it began to pump up and swell in size.

"Just finish him, already!" Ms. Naito ordered from her chair.

Steel Fist's bicep swelled even more as he cocked his arm further back behind his head.

"Steel Fist! What are you *doing*? Just finish him!" Ms. Naito yelled, growing concerned.

The bicep began to turn red hot and started viciously vibrating.

"He's going to take down the whole fucking building," Ms. Naito mumbled in disbelief.

She launched out of her chair, causing it to fall over backwards behind her. Her hands began to tremble in fear and her voice wavered as she yelled.

"Project Steel Fist, power down! Shut down code B-7-6-4-2!" Ms. Naito managed to shout over the sound of her heart pounding out of her chest.

The vibration of the arm increased in intensity as a light blue flame flickered around the bicep. The floor under his feet began to crack under the pressure of the building force. Steel Fist raised his head and looked directly at Ms. Naito through her shield.

"GRAYSON TOOK!"

The room seemed to freeze in time. The rhythmic, gyroscopic noises emanating from Steel Fist's bulging arm hit a peak. The elite guards frightfully looked on with wide eyes as Ms. Naito continued to frantically shriek Steel Fist's shutdown code. Grayson stared at Emily in her pod as the warmth from Steel Fist's charged-up arm crawled across his body. He closed his eyes and gripped the bracelet tightly.

Suddenly, the side wall exploded, sending large marble chunks flying across the room in a cloud of white dust. Faith shoulder-charged through the wall as the turbines on the back of her suit forcefully expelled blue, precise flames that propelled her forward at lightning-speed.

As she skimmed the ground through the cloud of dust, she performed a perfect downward draw-slash with an ignited, flaming, Onibi and completely sliced off a chunk of Steel Fist's back along with all of his Vax syringes. The force of the slash swept Steel Fist off his feet and caused him to crash into the ground like a felled tree.

Faith's metal feet sparked on the ground as she skidded to a halt like a practiced ice-skater. The elite guards were still gathering their bearings from Faith's explosive entrance as two rectangular multi-barrel rocket launchers extended over her head attached to mechanical arms.

Within her visor, Faith locked on to all six soldiers with her complete three-hundred and sixty-degree thermal view.

In rapid succession, twelve tiny missiles launched from her suit, leaving behind thin, white trails of swirling smoke in their wake. The small rockets impaled the soldiers in various parts of their bodies, two per soldier.

The guards looked at the rockets sticking in their bodies before they started to detonate in the order in which they hit. Bursting like potent firecrackers, the two side walls of the office splattered with blood, as limbs and chunks of flesh scattered the room. What remained of their tattered bodies lifelessly collapsed to the floor.

Ms. Naito dove under her desk, shaking and sweating like a wet leaf.

With her metallic feet clanking across the floor, Faith rushed over to Grayson, released the trigger on Onibi, and knelt next to him. Her visor retracted into her helmet as she placed her armored hand under Grayson's head.

She placed her other hand on Grayson's, which was still holding Emily's bracelet.

"Thought I lost you," Grayson mumbled, pushing through the pain.

Faith stroked the back of his head as she tried not to look at the wounds on his body.

"Never," Faith replied, cracking a smile as her eyes welled up.

Grayson nodded his head in Emily's direction.

"Get her out of here," Grayson pleaded as his eyes grew heavy.

Faith looked at her sweet daughter trapped in the stasis pod on the dolly and then at the clear shield in front of Ms. Naito's desk. Faith's visor shot back out into position, covering the top half of her face.

Ms. Naito reached toward her desk from the floor, but Faith fired another mini-missile at the overhead turret pointed at Emily, causing it to explode in a fireball of shrapnel. Ms. Naito's hand recoiled away from the desk as she was pelted with bits of hot, metal scraps.

With a single upward slice, Faith cut the shield and the desk in two with Onibi. The two halves of the desk melted away in a blue flame as Ms. Naito crawled backward on the floor like a frightened spider until her back rested against the wall.

Faith, towering over Ms. Naito, continued to approach. Her golden visor retracted into her helmet once more as she looked vengefully into Ms. Naito's petrified eyes.

"If- If you touch me," Ms. Naito started to stutter before Faith interrupted her.

"You fucked with the wrong girl," Faith firmly stated. "You can't win a battle by hiding behind a shield."

Faith slowly edged the tip of her flaming sword toward Ms. Naito's face. First, her bangs, eyebrows and eyelashes singed off of her face. As Faith moved the sword torturously closer, Ms. Naito began to scream and nonsensically beg.

The skin on her face began to bubble and melt as her teeth popped out of her mouth like popcorn kernels. Faith continued to press the blade into her head like soft butter causing the skin to peel away from the center of her face and revealing her meaty-red facial tendons and muscle tissue. Her eyes burst like volcanic pimples as her screams turned to gurgles.

Faith stopped applying pressure to the blade when she felt it hit the wall and Ms. Naito's melted head split in two. She released the trigger, which extinguished the flame and more clearly exposed Ms. Naito's corpse that now resembled a piece of damp, burnt broccoli wearing a charred white dress.

As she looked down at Ms. Naito's disfigured body, Faith felt a wave of relief as if she had finally squished a persistent cockroach. But, to her surprise, a part of her felt somewhat uneasy about the particularly slow and grisly nature of the death she had just caused.

The sound of a rapid "*clanking*" pierced Faith's ears from behind. Her visor shot down from her helmet as she turned around to face Steel Fist, who was pushing himself off the ground with his charged up and vibrating fist.

As he stood up and planted his feet on the ground in the center of the room, a cobalt blaze kindled on his back. Faith sheathed Onibi and approached him. Meeting him in the center of the room.

Steel Fist, breathing heavily, locked his arm into position as it quivered and pulsed with sparks shooting from the malfunctioning vents. He closed his fingers one at a time, each one clanging against his palm.

Faith calmly closed her fingers one at a time over the grip of her sword and twisted her feet into the ground.

She looked into his remaining robotic eye and felt a sense of calm wash over her.

Steel Fist mechanically released his eruptive punch like a space shuttle blasting off. Both hydraulic pistons extended and the vent flaps on his bicep opened as high-pressure flames burst from them.

Faith drew her katana, ignited it, and slashed faster than the eye could see. The edge of her blazing sword connected with the massive steel fist at the peak of its punch. As they both stood motionless for a heartbeat, Faith glanced at her sword to see the wire that housed Onibi's flame was completely dented to the side and the true blade of her sword had connected with the fiery fist.

She then watched as three cracks and a wave of energy traveled up Steel Fist's arm as her sword sliced through the entire length of the metallic limb.

A flash of blinding light filled the room as the massive, mechanical arm fractured and exploded. The entire exterior window was blown out in a blue pulse of energy as glass and rubble fell sixty-stories and peppered the streets of Red City.

Missing his arm, Steel Fist dropped to his knees with a heavy, resounding *thud.* His head hung low as his robotic eye flickered, seemingly staring at Ms. Naito's body.

"*Took…*" he said with a sad weakness to it.

Faith mercilessly slashed his other arm off and, with a clean cut, chopped through his neck. His head fell to the floor like a kettle bell as Faith raised Onibi over her head.

Putting all of the strength of her suit into her swing, she sliced down the middle of Steel Fist's body, implanting the flaming blade deep into the swirling energy source in his chest.

Growing unstable, rays of azure, volcanic flames sputtered from his torso. Faith urgently removed her sword and quickly sheathed it. Engaging her boosters to cross the room, she swiftly retrieved Emily's stasis pod, skated across the floor toward Grayson and heaved him over her shoulder. With flames spouting from the turbines on her back, she flew through the destroyed window.

Digging the claws on one of her hands into the side of the building, she skidded down the exterior of the skyscraper as the top floor detonated. A wave of energy traveled down the length of the building, shattering all of the windows, as Faith kicked off the building, vaulted the perimeter wall and boosted down the street. Shards of glass rained down on the street behind her until her suit began to "*beep*" and the words 'SHUT DOWN' flashed across her visor.

Grinding to a halt, Faith gently set Emily's stasis pod down in front of her and laid Grayson on the ground next to her. The visor on the suit went black and retracted into the helmet. The biomagnetic energy source on her sword and her suit flickered out and turned into dull, black spheres floating in place.

Fossilized in a frozen suit of armor, Faith looked at her innocent daughter's face and smiled, knowing, at the very least, she and Grayson had saved her life. She closed her eyes and saw a vision of her mother sitting in front of her cherry blossom painting, smiling back at her.

In the darkness, she heard the light squeal of brakes on a vehicle and smelled its thick, smokey exhaust.

"My god, they made it! Luden, help me put them in the car!"

Chapter 12

A Beautiful Morning

The worn tires of an rusty, red car with faded paint rolled through the muddy driveway of a seemingly abandoned farmhouse before slowing to a stop outside of a rotting barn.

The driver's door opened and Luden's polished, black boot sunk into cakey muck as he exited the vehicle.

He closed his eyes for a moment and flared his nostrils before deciding to let it go. As he closed the door behind him, he surveyed the winding road behind him, listening and looking for signs of being followed.

Satisfied, he removed a small box wrapped in newspaper from the back seat of the car and approached the worn-down barn.

As he arrived at the doors, he wiped his foot across a patch of grass in an attempt to remove the sticky mud from his boot. Above the barn door sat a surveillance camera and an intercom.

Luden quick-drew a finger gun and pointed it at the camera.

"Pew!" he said as he mimicked firing it.

"You're good," Kurt's voice rang out from the intercom.

Luden opened the creaky door and entered a completely barren barn. As he scanned the interior, he noticed several explosive devices rigged on the walls and ceiling.

In the center of the barn was a spray-painted mark of a red crow with barbed wire encircling it on the floor. Dust puffed from underneath his muddy boots as he walked toward it.

He stopped just short of the crow and the flooring raised an inch before parting, revealing a lengthy staircase down.

At the bottom of the staircase was a stark, white hallway with a steel door at the end. On the door was a red, Bio-Yomi arch with a big red 'X' spray-painted over it.

Luden reached the door, brushed some dirt from his black turtle neck and rapped his knuckles on thick steel.

A heavy lock turned over and the hefty door slowly opened, revealing Grayson and a messy workshop behind him.

"I'm glad you could make it, come on in," Grayson said through a warm smile.

"What can I say, the kiddo loves me. My conscience wouldn't let me miss it," Luden replied, rubbing the back of his head.

"Uncle Luden!" a tiny voice yelled from behind Grayson.

As Grayson closed and locked the vault-like door behind Luden, little Emily scuttled across the room and slammed into his leg, giving it a big hug.

"Here," Luden whispered to Grayson, handing him the newspaper-wrapped present over Emily's head.

Grayson reached out a mechanical prosthetic arm and accepted the gift.

Luden knelt down to Emily and delivered a warm smile.

"You know, I'm giving out free piggyback rides today… but only to birthday girls…" Luden said teasingly to Emily.

"It's my birthday, it's my birthday!" Emily quickly informed him through a huge smile.

"I guess you're in luck then, here we go!"

Luden scooped Emily up and tossed her over his back for a ride. As he stood up, Emily giggled with joy.

"I don't know why she likes you," Grayson said shaking his head.

"Grayson, you're the only one who *doesn't* like me," Luden said jokingly. "I'm glad to see you're looking better, man."

"Kurt's doctor friend does good work, I miss the arm, but it looks like the leg is here to stay," Grayson replied.

"And… Faith?" Luden asked as Emily tugged the hair on his head.

"She's… adjusting. But she's hanging in there. Come on in, she's just about done with the cake," Grayson responded.

As they walked through the workshop, Luden noticed pieces of the Izanami suit disassembled on a work bench surrounded by tools, a blowtorch, and a welder's mask.

They made their way to a repurposed breakroom with a dining table in the middle of it. Kurt sat on a stool at the table, drawing up some schematics. He looked up as Luden entered the room with Emily's head peeking over his shoulder.

"My god, Luden. You become leader of the Pyschophants, and a few months later you've aged five years," Kurt said through a smirk.

"They say you are a product of the people you spend the most time around… And I have been spending a lot of time around a wrinkly info broker," Luden poked back as he set Emily down on the floor.

Faith appeared in the doorway holding a sloppy-looking chocolate cake with her two robotic, prosthetic arms.

"All right, Em! It's ready," Faith lovingly exclaimed.

She slowly and carefully walked toward the table on two mechanical prosthetic legs as the cake wobbled in her arms. Luden reached out to support her.

"Here, let me…" Luden began to say.

"If you lay that hand on me, Luden, you won't get it back. I can do it," Faith said as she reached the table and set the cake down.

Scribbled in blue frosting on the top of the cake was: *Happy 3rd Birthday Emily*

They all took their seats at the table and sang 'Happy Birthday' to Emily as she clapped her hands and emitted a contagious smile. Grayson, Faith, Luden, Kurt, and Emily finally enjoyed a moment of peace as they indulged in a truly delicious cake.

Epilogue
Aftershock

Hirohiko Naito, a stern man with a scowl and a pitted face sat in a magnificent office with his hands clasped together and his elbows on his desk.

Two guards outfitted in advanced prosthetic limbs and tactical gear tossed a filthy man in a lab coat onto the floor in front of him. One of the guards approached Mr. Naito's desk and set a data chip down in front of him.

A bloodied Dr. Borka pushed himself off the floor onto his knees and looked at Mr. Naito through swollen black eyes.

"What is this?" Mr. Naito questioned him with a commanding presence.

Dr. Borka shook his head as his bottom lip quivered in fear.

One of the guards placed a pistol to the back of Borka's head and nudged him with the muzzle.

"It is… the data from Red City. All of the video footage and research data from online storage. Including… the footage from Ms. Naito's office."

"This will explain why the building collapsed? And what my… daughter… was hiding?" Mr. Naito queried numbly.

"Yes," Borka whispered in defeat. "But I do not think you will like what you see..."

"Remove him," Mr. Naito ordered his guards.

The guards grabbed the beaten Borka under his arms and dragged his limp body out of the office. A trail of Borka's spattered blood stained an ornate rug on their way out.

Mr. Naito picked up the translucent data chip and gripped it tightly with his fingertips. The stone-faced man's pitted cheek twitched as he distantly stared at the chip-slot on his desk.

www.ingramcontent.com/pod-product-compliance
Lightning Source LLC
LaVergne TN
LVHW051005080826
845145LV00009B/2472

* 9 7 8 1 7 3 6 5 6 5 7 0 4 *